DIADEM
Worlds of Magic

John Peel is the author of numerous best-selling novels for young adults, including installments in the Star Trek, Are You Afraid of the Dark?, and Where in the World is Carmen Sandiego? series. He is also the author of many acclaimed novels of science fiction, horror, and suspense.

Mr. Peel currently lives on the outer rim of the Diadem, on a planet popularly known as Earth.

Book of Names

John Peel

2004
Llewellyn Publications
St. Paul, Minnesota 55164-0383, U.S.A.

First Llewellyn Edition
First printing, 2004

Previously published in 1997 by Scholastic, Inc.

Cover design by Gavin Dayton Duffy
Cover illustration © 2004 by Bleu Turrell/Artworks
All interior illustrations reprinted by permission of Scholastic, Inc.

Project management and editing by Andrew Karre

Library of Congress Cataloging-in-Publication Data
Peel, John, 1954–
Book of Names / John Peel.—1st Llewellyn Edition
p. cm.—(Diadem, worlds of magic; #1)
Summary: Score, Renald, and Pixel are snatached from different worlds and taken by Bestials to the planet Treen where they are to be offered as sacrifice.
ISBN: 0-7387-0617-5
[1. Magic—Fiction. 2. Fantasy.] I. Title.
PZ7.P348Bo 2004
[Fic]—dc22 2004040878

Llewellyn Publications
A Division of Llewellyn Worldwide, Ltd.
P.O. Box 64383
St. Paul, MN 55164-0383, U.S.A.
www.llewellyn.com

Printed in the United States of America

Other Diadem books by John Peel

#2 *Book of Signs*

#3 *Book of Magic*

#4 *Book of Thunder*

#5 *Book of Earth*

#6 *Book of Nightmares*

#7 *Book of War*

For my nephews, Jonathan and Simon,
and for my niece and goddaughter, Alison

PROLOGUE

The Shadows were out hunting, far from home. In a pack, they moved through the spaces between the many worlds, seeking their prey. It couldn't just be anyone. It had to be the right victim.

The correct sacrifice. They all anticipated the thrill of the hunt and the final taking. This was not merely their job. It was their sport. It was their pleasure. They enjoyed finding their targets, and they felt a genuine thrill as their victim was dragged off to its fate.

The Shadows' not-quite-faces seemed to wrinkle with laughter and pleasure. As they closed in on one small, green-and-blue planet, they could feel that this was the one. Here they would find their next victim.

Here, on a small, backward, off-the-beaten-path planet named Earth.

Here the right prey lived—for the moment. Sliding unseen and unsuspected into the atmosphere of the planet, they began to close in on their chosen target. They left a trail of chilled air behind them, like the contrails of a jet aircraft, as they spiraled down, down, down toward the waiting land below.

All their senses felt as if they were on fire. Over the ocean they sped, zeroing in on one small island. A tiny place called Manhattan, perched on a small rock above the surface of the Atlantic Ocean. There they would find the right person. There the sacrifice awaited.

They were ready and eager. Soon, very soon, they could take their prey . . .

1

Score was scared. It was the one emotion he knew really well. He'd lived with it for most of his short life. He reckoned he must have been born scared, because he couldn't ever recall spending a single day when he wasn't afraid.

It had been his father, mostly, who had scared Score. Tony Caruso was a mean, tough guy, and, even on the streets, the word had been out that nobody messed with Tony Caruso and lived to brag about it. His was a name that, even whispered, scared gang members, mobsters, and even cops all over Lower Manhattan. Tony Caruso was Bad, and the capital letter was there as a warning.

Then, just two weeks ago, everything had changed. Bad Tony had done something wrong, again, but this time the police took him away. Usually, he managed to pay off someone or to get away from the police somehow. But not this time. He'd slipped up, and the police had solid evidence on him. Score didn't much care, as long as they kept his father away from him for a long, long time.

Score found himself alone, going through everything in their small apartment. He managed to find some money that Bad Tony had hidden. Then, behind a loose board in Bad Tony's bedroom, he found a letter that had never been mailed. On the front was his name and address. Puzzled, he stared at it. The handwriting looked familiar, but it wasn't his father's . . .

It was his mother's! She'd been dead for three years, but Score remembered her well. She'd been another of Bad Tony's victims, another reason to hate his father. Excitement mounted in Score as he opened the envelope and took out the sheet of paper within. Unfolding it, he began to read.

you are 1
of
♀ne two
K
+Adam
Treen is the
start
past
future
banished from the cent
e became children onc

It made no sense to him whatsoever. Some of it seemed to make sense, but really didn't. "Treen is the start," for example. Who or what was Treen? And what was he, she, or it the start of? Score simply didn't understand. Why would his mother want him to have something like this, something he couldn't understand? She must have hidden it for him to find one day. If she felt it was important, maybe he'd figure out what it meant somehow. He carefully folded it and slipped it into the wallet of money he had found. With the money, he planned to start a new, improved life . . .

Then the police had taken Score, as well.

Not under arrest. Well, they hadn't called it that, but he had been taken in front of a judge, who'd placed him in the custody of the Children's Services people. It wasn't arrest because they claimed to be doing everything for his own good—including locking him up when he had tried to escape. But this time, he'd not only tried, he'd succeeded.

So, now he was back where he belonged, on the Bowery, in New York City. Score was scared here, too, but at least he knew the streets and the dangers. There were gangs to watch out for, and other people might hold his father's actions against him. But at least he had a chance, since he was on his own turf.

There was another thing that was scaring him, and one he had no control over. For the past week, he'd been having a recurring dream. It confused and worried him, because it made absolutely no sense. He would hear, over and over again, a repeated tune. It wasn't anything he'd ever heard before, or anything he'd ever choose to listen to. It was slow and kind of mournful, the kind of music you might hear at a funeral—like at his mother's funeral. He couldn't get the tune out of his mind.

The dream always ended in a flash of green light, pulsing slightly, drawing him toward it. The light was like a promise, a beacon. Score always reached for it, wanting it so that he could be rich and happy forever. But when he touched it, he felt an abrupt shock. He would immediately wake up, shaking and sweating.

Why was he having this dream over and over? Was he sick? Or was it maybe some kind of warning? He didn't really believe in dreams being able to warn you, but this bothered him. Maybe it was a warning. But about what?

His stomach growled, reminding him that he needed food. He had a few dollars left from the money he'd managed to scrape together, but he'd need a lot more to survive on his own. There was no point in going back to the crummy apartment he'd lived in until two weeks ago. Too many bad memories hung over that place. There were probably other people living there now, and, besides, the police would be bound to look for him there. He had no place to call home anymore.

He needed money, and that meant only one possibility. There was one thing that Score was really good at—scamming the scam artists. They worked the streets, picking on tourists, and trying to get money away from them. Score's favorite was the old three-card monte. The scam artist would have three cards, facedown. One was always the queen of spades. To win money, the tourist had to guess which card was the queen. They never managed it, of course, because usually the scammer palmed the card and replaced it with a different one. Somehow, though, that never happened with Score. He always managed to pick the right card. As a result, he could win money, but he had to be careful never to hit the same street dealer twice.

Luck was with him. He found a tall, hyperactive hustler working one of the streets on the edge of Chinatown, keeping up a stream of patter, jokes, and wide grins as he shuffled and twisted his three cards on a small table. "C'mon," he begged the passing tourists. "It's easy, don't ya see? Just pick the queen, and I give you twenty dollars. Only five dollars to try. C'mon, you can do it . . ."

"I can," Score said, confidently taking out his last five and placing it on the table.

"All right!" the dealer exclaimed, obviously figuring he was reeling in a sucker. "Here ya go, my man. Watch the cards carefully."

Score didn't bother. He didn't need to try and follow those flying fingers as they shuffled the three cards. A couple of curious tourists stopped to watch, smiling at him from behind their cameras.

"Now, which one is it?" the dealer asked, grinning. Everyone watched as Score paused.

It was mostly for show. Score knew which card it was. He didn't know how; he just knew. "This one," he said, seeing the momentary flare of triumph in his opponent's eyes, knowing Score was wrong.

Score turned over the queen of spades.

The wide grin vanished. "Huh?"

"Twenty dollars," Score said, holding out the card to the startled cheat. The man looked like he was going to complain, but the tourists were laughing and encouraging Score. The dealer couldn't afford to alienate potential victims.

"Well done, my man," he said, trying to put on a good face. He peeled a bill from a roll in his pocket and handed it across. He was still obviously unsure how Score had done what he'd done. "Want to try again, double or quits?"

"Sure," agreed Score. The growing crowd laughed and encouraged him.

The dealer's hands flew like lightning this time, but not fast enough to confuse Score.

"That one," Score said, confidently. He reached for the card he'd indicated, but the dealer beat him to it this time, eyes grinning as he flipped over the card he knew couldn't be—

The queen of spades!

The crowd had held its breath, and now started to applaud. The dealer looked stunned, and then ready to kill. But he had no option since everyone was watching. He peeled off another bill and handed it over.

"Again?" Score jeered.

The man wanted to refuse. He didn't understand what was happening here. Neither did the crowd, which was now about twenty strong. But they were on the side of the underdog, the kid who was winning at the game. And if the dealer backed down, he might as well go home. He'd get no money from them. But if he agreed, and somehow, *impossibly*, Score won again . . .

"How are you doing it, kid?" he asked, playing for time.

"Luck," Score suggested.

A new voice, mellow and amused, came from over his shoulder.

It is not luck, but skill, my friend
That leads to winning in the end.

"Huh?" Score turned around to see who was speaking in rhymes to him. His eyes opened wide at the sight of the tall man. He was dressed entirely in black—shirt, trousers, boots. His hair was black, and his pale skin seemed to . . . flicker.

"Who are you?" Score asked. The man looked outrageous, and yet . . . yet there was something somehow familiar about him. Like he'd met the man before. Maybe he was an "associate" of Bad Tony.

Call me LeCora if you will
And I'll explain your special skill.

The weird man reached over to the table where the monte dealer's cards were. He turned to look Score carefully in the face.

There is one thing I must reveal
The gift you have is very real,
The black queen goes just where you choose
With magic you can never lose.

As he spoke, he turned over all the cards on the table.

They were all the queen of spades.

Nobody watching understood what was going on, least of all Score. How could that be? He only picked one card . . . LeCora saw his astonishment, and explained again:

The power to change things in small ways
Will be with you for all your days.

Score began to understand, despite the man's rather roundabout way of explaining things. He didn't have the power to pick where the card was—he had the ability to change any card he picked into the queen of spades.

"Hey," the dealer growled angrily. "You been ripping me off, kid!" He lunged for Score and the money.

Score's fingers clutched his forty-five dollars and he whirled and ran for his life, dodging through the crowd. The dealer, yelling furiously, tried to follow. But he was larger, and the crowd didn't part for him.

Once Score was sure he'd escaped the monte dealer, he slowed down and then stood, panting in a side street. That had been close, but he was free again—and now with money in his pocket! Score still didn't understand what had happened—the appearance of the flickering man, the business with the cards . . .

Was it possible that the stranger was right? That somehow Score had the power to change small things? He didn't know, but there was one real easy way to find out. His fingers closed in on the five-dollar bill in his pocket. If he could change an ace to the queen of spades, then this should be just as easy. Unsure of what to do, Score simply closed his eyes and concentrated, and then withdrew the five-dollar bill from his pocket. He crumpled it, and then stared down at it.

Ben Franklin's face stared back at him . . . *All right!* Score felt excited, confused, and a bit scared. He'd changed a five-dollar bill into a hundred just by thinking about it. How, he had no idea. But he had done it once—and could do it again, whenever he felt like it.

Score felt like a winner, at last . . .

Above Score, unseen in the air, the Shadows hovered.

There was their victim, ready and waiting, and all alone.

Together, they laughed and then plunged earthward, seeking out host bodies. This far from the center, they were invisible. They needed other people to do their work for them. Still, that was no real problem. It had been planned, after all . . . There, in the next block over, was a gang of street thugs, showing off their knives. It took mere seconds for the Shadows to slip within their bodies and their minds. Then they informed their unwitting hosts about the presence of one small, weedy boy with money just a block away . . .

The gang began to move without a word.

Score grinned to himself as he turned the two twenties into hundred-dollar bills. Not a bad salary, for ten seconds of work. Five dollars into three hundred, just like that. No more scrimping and begging and stealing for him. Just . . .

He suddenly realized he was not alone. The street he was in was narrow, with sky-high buildings cramped together on either side. Trash cans, bags of half-open garbage, and abandoned boxes littered the street. And at the far end, a gang of seven young men suddenly appeared. There were glints of silver that were obviously knives, and Score realized he was in serious trouble. The boys belonged to the Zaps, one of the most dangerous of the street gangs in this area. Score didn't belong to any gangs. For one thing, he was too young to join them. For another, they scared him. But not belonging to a gang meant you were fair game if one of them caught you on their turf.

Like these Zaps had just caught him.

"Uh, hey," Score said weakly. The gang members said nothing, just moved slowly, purposefully, toward him.

There was something wrong with their eyes. They looked entirely black, as if someone had spilled paint into them. And their faces were expressionless, which made it even scarier. Normally, they would be laughing and taunting their victim before jumping him.

They'd steal whatever he had that was worth their while—his three hundred dollars!—and then rough him up a bit.

But their faces were all wrong, their weapons held too ready for that. These punks weren't going to rob him. They were going to kill him.

There was no choice left for him. Score whirled around and ran for his life. The gang members raced after him in concentrated silence.

The short street led to another, and Score hurriedly dashed down it. There was nobody around to help, just a couple of derelicts drinking from bottles in paper bags and ignoring the world in a self-induced haze. Panicking, his legs tiring, his lungs on fire, Score whipped around the next corner and into another street. He heard the gang's footsteps close behind him.

He knew he was in really serious trouble.

This street ended in a blockade, topped with barbed wire. Beyond it lay the East River. There were no other turnoffs, nowhere to look for a hiding place. Score was trapped. A dead end.

He turned, and the gang was there. Their weapons at the ready, they slowly advanced on him . . .

Now! It was time. The Shadows could feel the surge of energy. They could also taste the delicious fear radiating from their target as their host bodies closed in.

And then it happened.

Score whirled around as there was an explosion of sound from behind him, behind the East River barricade. His jaw fell open at what he saw. He was unable to move, stunned by the shape that hurled from the water, into the air, to fly over the top of a ten-foot barrier without trouble. Even drenched by the tremendous splash, Score just stood, shocked senseless, and stared.

It was a killer whale. Maybe twenty feet long, black, with a white underbelly and patches of white on its sleek, dark skin.

What was a killer whale doing in the East River?

Or, more accurately, leaping out of it?

The huge beast opened its wide jaws as it hurtled down from the top of its arc, toward the ground.

Then things got really weird.

It began to shrink, growing legs and arms. Just when it looked as if it would hit the road, the whale somehow morphed into a roughly human form, landing lightly on two muscular legs. The man—if that's what it was—stood over seven feet tall and looked strong and very, very dangerous. He was still black, with a white stomach and blotches.

"Back!" the creature howled at the gang members, who had watched in stunned silence. Then he turned to Score and beckoned, "To me, if you want to save your miserable life!"

Score was scared of the big man and was still shaken and confused by what he had seen. But he wasn't stupid, and knew that his only chance of survival here was to do as the creature had suggested. Quickly, he ran to stand behind him.

It was time. The Shadows suddenly leaped with one mind out of their host bodies, freeing the gang members to do as they willed. Hovering unseen above, the Shadows watched what happened next . . .

The gang members looked as though they were waking up from some kind of nightmare. Life suddenly returned to them as their eyes became normal again. Then they stared in horror at the beast defending Score, as if they hadn't seen him before and had no idea what was going on.

"Back!" the stranger commanded. "This boy is under my protection."

"Yeah?" whispered Score, still not certain he trusted the stranger. "And just who . . . what are you?"

"I am S'hee," the whatever-he-was answered, as if that were enough.

It wasn't—not for the gang, at least. Despite their shock, they all screamed and tried to jump the creature at once.

Like lightning, S'hee was on them, kicking and punching with incredible strength and skill. Score couldn't even make out what has happening, S'hee moved that fast. Score saw one gang member go down, his arm clearly broken, his knife rattling away.

The toughs pulled back after their first attack failed. The one boy was down, moaning, with his broken arm. Two of the others had long cuts across exposed skin, and one held his left arm, clearly in pain. S'hee was untouched, but panting slightly. He'd done very well so far, but he was still unarmed and all the gang had knives.

Then one of them drew a large, silver pistol.

"Let's go," S'hee yelled. With his left arm, he scooped Score up without effort. With his right, he ripped at the strands of wire, tearing a hole in the fence. As the gun fired, Score heard the first bullet narrowly miss them. Then S'hee was on the barrier, and he tensed for a second before throwing himself and Score forward, toward the waiting East River.

The gang members dashed forward, furious that their prey was escaping. Two of them managed to mount the barrier and stare down at the river. Their faces were filled with confusion and shock.

There had been no splash as their targets hit the water. And, as they stared down, they could see that the water was still, lapping gently against the rocks. There was no sign of anyone having entered the water at all. And no sign of the black-and-white creature or the boy.

They had vanished, completely and mysteriously . . . but how?

And . . . to where?

2

The Shadows were quite pleased with what they had done and whispered amongst themselves as they passed beyond Earth again. Their victim had been taken, as had been planned, and now it was time to seek their second target. They slipped through the barriers between the worlds, this time coming upon one that seemed to be mostly islands in large, dark oceans. This was the world known as Ordin. Once again, they flew down, unseen, through the atmosphere, heading for the largest of the islands, where their next victim lived, unsuspecting of her fate . . .

Helaine Votrin was angrier than she had ever been before. She stared across the room in the enormous, stone-walled castle. For a moment, she was absolutely speechless, which was a rare state for her. Her father—tall, muscular, dark-bearded, dark-eyed—stared back evenly at her from his seat. He was dressed in his formal clothes, not his warrior's outfit, but he was quite clearly in a fight right now with his youngest daughter.

"You must be joking," was finally all that Helaine could think of saying.

"Of course I'm not joking," Lord Votrin snapped back peevishly. "This is much too important a matter to make jests about. And it's not something I care to discuss."

"But . . ." Helaine loved her father, but right now she wished she could take a sword to him. "I'm too young to be married!"

"You are twelve years old," her father replied firmly. "It's legal for you to be betrothed at eight, should I decide it. You're quite old enough to get married, and

I say you will be married to Dathan Peverel. And, as I said before, I do not care to discuss this any further."

"You want to ruin my entire life and then not even talk about it?" Helaine demanded.

"I am not ruining your life," her father said, clearly struggling to keep his temper. "You would have to be married off sooner or later. I have simply decided that now is the perfect time. Lord Peverel and I are both in agreement on the matter. Our houses need to be joined, and a marriage between his oldest son and my only unmarried daughter is the prefect way to do it."

"It's not perfect for me!" Helaine raged. "Everybody knows that Dathan Peverel is an absolute idiot and a fop! He's not the kind of person I'd choose to marry—if I wanted to marry yet, which I don't."

This was too much for her father. Rising to his feet, he slammed his fist down on the table, almost splintering the wood. "Enough!" he thundered. "You will do as you are told. You are going to marry young Peverel. You'd marry him even if he were a drooling half-wit, if I order it. You have absolutely no say in the matter."

"You would treat me so badly?" Helaine asked, disgusted to find herself on the verge of tears.

"I will treat you any way I please," her father answered gruffly. Then he took a deep breath and tried to be reasonable. "It is within my legal powers to marry you off when I choose and to whom I choose. I'm sorry that Peverel is such a sad case, but it can't be helped. Both our families need this alliance. The Border Lords are getting discontented again, and it may lead to skirmishes or even war. Peverel and I must pool our resources to prevent this, and your marriage will be the ideal way to cement our alliance." His voice softened slightly. "And look on the bright side. Dathan is bound to let you do anything you want, so you'll probably be running him and his castle in next to no time."

Helaine refused to be mollified. "Oh, fine!" she snapped. "I'm supposed to be comforted by the fact that I'll be able to boss an idiot husband around?"

"You will do as you are told," Lord Votrin informed her coldly. "You are to be wed tomorrow afternoon. The guests are already on their way, including one or two of the Border Lords I want a look at. Now, you may go to your room and think about what I have said.

"Tomorrow?" echoed Helaine, aghast. "That's impossible! I—"

"You will do as you are told!" her father yelled again, his thinly stretched patience finally breaking. "Now, go to you room, or I'll have one of my guards carry you there and lock you in!"

It was impossible to argue further. Helaine turned her back on her father and marched out of his audience room. *I will not cry!* she told herself sternly. *And I will not obey.*

Helaine needed to get the anger out of her system before she could think clearly. One thing she was absolutely certain of was that she was not going to marry anyone tomorrow—least of all Dathan Peverel!

Back in her room, she unlaced the large, flowing dress that she wore. She hated having to wear this cumbersome thing. It must have been designed by a man for the sole purpose of making sure that a woman couldn't move about properly. It was supposed to look pretty, but Helaine had no love for that kind of beauty. Only things that did their jobs well could be beautiful. A dress like this was more like wearing chains than clothing, and she tolerated it only when she had to.

Helaine went to the small chest of clothes she kept hidden under her bed. Nobody, not even her favorite maid, Retlyn, was allowed to see this chest, because it contained her greatest secret. She only dared bring it out when she was alone. Inside it were a pair of breeches, a pair of soft leather boots, a heavy woolen tunic, and a cap. Quickly, she dressed herself and examined her reflection in the polished metal mirror she kept on her dressing table.

Perfect. With her long hair pinned up under the heavy cap and the loose tunic over her upper body, she looked like any other youngster in the castle. Any other *male* youngster.

This was completely forbidden, of course. Women—and especially young girls—had strictly defined places in Ordin society. Women were supposed to learn sewing, sometimes reading, cooking, and other "gentle" arts. Boys, on the other hand, could do whatever they pleased. Helaine had started this off as something of a game at first, when she was about five years old. But when she discovered that nobody recognized the small, scruffy-looking "Renald" as being the same person as the somewhat regal and aristocratic Helaine Votrin, she had become addicted to her disguise.

Only one person knew about it, and she had sworn him to absolute secrecy. This was Borigen, Lord

Votrin's oldest and most loyal soldier. Borigen had been shocked at first when he'd accidentally stumbled across her secret, but he was very fond of her, and she'd managed to persuade him to go along with her and keep her secret safe.

He'd agreed reluctantly, and then tried to talk her out of it. All of the boys in the castle, he'd pointed out, had to learn to fight. If "Renald" didn't, then there would be trouble, and she'd be found out anyway. He'd obviously hoped to scare her into quitting. It hadn't worked. Helaine had always known her own abilities.

"Fine," she told him. "Then I shall learn to fight, too."

Borigen had been very reluctant to agree to that, and she knew he'd only agreed eventually because he thought she'd do so badly that she'd be given a hiding and then give up in disgust.

Only, it hadn't worked like that at all. And now, seven years later, "Renald" stepped carefully out of Helaine's room and headed for the practice area in the courtyard below. Pausing at the gateway, she greeted one of the guards as she strapped on her practice sword.

The guard grinned back. "Come to show 'em how it should be done, hey?" he asked, winking. "Don't be too hard on 'em."

"I'll try to behave," Renald replied. "But I'm in a bad mood and want to get it out of me."

"Uh-oh," the guard muttered, his eyes twinkling in anticipation. "Sounds like somebody's going to get his head whacked."

"It won't be me," Renald answered confidently.

"I never thought it would be." The guard shook his own head. "Go easy, though. You don't need to really kill 'em."

"Probably not," agreed Renald. Stepping outside, Renald headed for the practice lines. There were several other young men around, all working with their practice swords. Borigen was off to one side, showing two of the younger boys how to fight with the dull-edged swords. Renald's eyes scanned the ranks and lighted on Mardren. Perfect! He was such a pompous jerk, and needed to be taken down a peg or two.

Mardren was the son of her father's advisor and thought he was much better bred than any of the other boys—especially Renald. Borigen had explained Renald away as the son of a cousin of his, and therefore fairly low in the pecking order. As Renald, Helaine had been bullied a bit to begin with, until she had shown everyone the foolishness of this approach. Now, most of them were pretty wary of her—that is, of Renald. Except Mardren, who never seemed to learn.

"Want to be beaten today?" he sneered, seeing Renald approaching.

"Think you can do it?" asked Renald, calmly. "Then try."

With a scornful grin, Mardren raised his own practice sword and lunged for his intended target. The swords didn't have points, and their edges were deliberately dulled so that they couldn't draw blood. But they could and did leave bruises where the blows landed with sufficient force. The idea was to become proficient with real swords, without actually killing. Hurting was another matter entirely. Borigen felt that the bruises were a wonderful incentive to make the boys (and Helaine) become better fighters.

Renald twisted slightly to avoid the thrust, whipping up her sword in response and batting Mardren's aside with casual ease. Mardren was all arrogance and little skill. In the past, Renald had generally gone easy on him, not wishing to make an enemy of the other youth.

But today she simply didn't care. As Mardren was over-balanced slightly from his thrust, she whacked him hard on his left arm with her own blade as she spun about.

Mardren grimaced with pain, but he was too proud to cry out. Instead, he attacked her again, this time with anger to add to his arrogance. But it couldn't match the anger in her heart, and she fought back. He never managed to touch her once with his blade, but she tapped him easily another three times in quick succession. The other boys had grown silent, watching this fight. They all knew Renald was the best sword fighter in the group, and that Mardren was going to get a drubbing he'd remember painfully for days. Renald didn't care. She flicked her sword out again, slapping it against Mardren's left thigh. She was deliberately going for places to hurt him, to provoke him into continuing the fight.

Borigen moved forward, obviously aware of what was happening. Renald knew better than to take her eyes off Mardren to look at her instructor, but she knew Borigen was going to stop the fight. He'd obviously realized what she was doing.

"No," said a familiar, commanding voice. "Let them fight. In a real battle, you can't just call off an opponent."

It was her father! He must have come out to watch the training. Renald chanced a quick glance and saw her father watching from a doorway, his arms folded grimly across his chest. Then she caught sight of Mardren's blade flickering for her face and barely avoided the thrust.

That was a dirty blow—not actually illegal, since anything fighters did to win was okay, but the students were warned not to go for the face. It was always possible to blind someone accidentally, even with practice swords. Mardren obviously wanted to hurt his opponent rather than win fairly—which he had probably guessed by now he couldn't do.

Renald's anger grew even more at this, and she simply stopped holding back. She whirled about, parrying his next attack, and then countered with a blow to his stomach that left him wheezing slightly. A tap on the sword arm, as he hesitated, then a slap against the side of his neck. That would leave a visible bruise for a week, a reminder to all of what he'd suffered. Then a twist and into his heart. If these had been real swords, Mardren would be dead, and everyone knew it. As it was, the thump of the blade against his chest would make him sore whenever he breathed.

"It's over," Borigen said flatly, without even looking at the watching lord.

Renald nodded and dropped her practice sword to the ground. She started to turn when Mardren snarled and lunged for her with his own sword upraised, aimed again for her face. Renald moved to one side, brought up her hands, and gripped Mardren's wrist as he missed her face. Then, feeling anger and exultation both at the same time, she whirled about and used her grip to throw Mardren over her shoulder and heavily to the ground. As she released his wrist, it twisted sharply. Mardren let out a thin, reedy cry of pain as he hit the ground.

"Nicely done," Borigen admitted as he brushed angrily past her. "It's unfortunate his wrist is broken. He'll be useless for weeks."

"He's been useless all his life," Renald murmured, not at all bothered by what she'd done. She turned to find her father staring down at her, an expression she'd never seen before in his eyes. For a second Renald panicked that he had seen through her disguise, but then his hand clapped her shoulder, and she realized that the expression in his eyes was approval.

"Nicely done, lad," Lord Votrin complimented her. "You show a great deal of skill with the sword. And without. You'll no doubt make a fine fighting man one of these days."

No fighting man shall this one be,
But as a warrior, best of three.

A strange voice spoke from behind them. Renald twisted and stared at a man she had never seen before. He was dressed in black, with dark hair and pale skin. There was something just vaguely familiar about him that she couldn't place . . .

"Who are you?" Lord Votrin asked the stranger.

Call me Cleora, my good lord.
I came to watch her splendid sword.

Lord Votrin was obviously very confused. "What are you talking about?" he demanded. "What *her?*"

The stranger leaned forward to gesture at Renald.

Renald foresees an opponent's move,
A power that lets her skill improve.
But this Renald is in disguise,
And now you must believe your eyes.
This youth is one you can't explain,
Renald's your daughter, fair Helaine.

Renald stared at the stranger in horror, realizing that he had just betrayed her. She started to turn and run, but her father's strong hand caught her arm and held her firm. He glared at Renald, then at Cleora. "I don't know who you are, but we shall soon see what truth there is in your strange words." His free hand ripped the cap from Renald's head, and Helaine's long hair came tumbling down about her shaking shoulders.

Lord Votrin's face went white and then red as he realized whom he held in his grip. "Helaine!" he gasped, shocked and furious in equal measures.

"Father," she admitted, holding her head up proudly, refusing to avoid his glare. "I am the best swordsman here."

Her father was shaking. "Enough!" he snarled. "Haven't you shamed me enough already?"

"A moment ago, you were praising me," she reminded him.

"A moment ago, I did not know who you were," he replied grimly. "Now I do. Go to your room and stay there, before I order you locked in."

"Very well," she agreed. She bent to pick up her cap, and then shook his hand free. Without another word, she walked back through the shocked ranks of her fellow students. Former fellow students, she realized. There was no way her father would allow her to continue her training now. Not that there was that much left for her to learn.

As she entered her room, Helaine slammed the door and started to remove her tunic. She might as well get out of these things. She'd never be allowed to wear them again. Damn that Cleora! He'd somehow known her secret and betrayed her.

Then she stopped and replaced the tunic. Changing back into her dress would be to admit to her father that he had won. She wouldn't do it. This might be her last defiant act, but she would never become the meek girl he wanted to order around. Whether he liked it or not, she was Renald, the best swordsperson in the castle. And she'd sooner die than marry that oaf Dathan!

Or sooner run away . . .

The idea formed suddenly, and then it made a great deal of sense. Why stay here to be traded off like a sack of flour or a tankard of ale? She could get out of the castle and go off alone. It wouldn't be safe for a solitary girl, but if she stayed disguised as Renald, she should be fine. And with her skills, she would probably be accepted as a soldier in training at another castle . . . The more she thought about it, the better she liked the plan. She was not staying here any longer. Her best bet would be to leave by night, under cover of darkness. She could slip over the wall and away before she was missed. By the time anyone came to look for her, she'd be long gone.

She didn't dare try to steal a horse, though she could ride one without trouble. A horse could be traced too easily. On foot it would be harder, but safer.

She'd need a sword, which wasn't a problem. She fished under her bed for the one she'd convinced Borigen to give her a year ago. She'd kept it polished and sharpened, so there was no problem there. She also took out her knife, which slipped in the top of her right boot. She'd need a bow and arrow, which she'd have to take from the armory before she left. And food and a water skin. Aside from that, all she needed now was the night.

Assuming her father didn't send for her before that.

While Helaine waited, her mind flitted back and forth on a number of things. Cleora, for one. How had he seen through her disguise? And why had he betrayed her? And that comment of his that she could somehow foresee where a blow was coming from. What nonsense! And yet . . . she *had* somehow seen it when Mardren had tried to stab her face, hadn't she? And in time to stop it. Maybe there was more to this than she'd ever realized before . . .

Her mind drifted, and she remembered something else odd from these past few days. She'd been having a recurring dream in which she was in some sort of library. She'd been hunting for a book, which she'd finally found and started reading. It was filled with cryptic symbols and signs. Between the pages of the book was another page, pressed like a leaf. It glowed blue, dazzling her eyes. Helaine wanted more than anything else to see this page and the words it held. But every time she reached for it, she woke up.

She'd had this dream every night for the past five days. Normally, she couldn't remember much about her dreams, but this was as vivid as it was mysterious. She kept thinking about it—even when she should have been planning her escape.

Finally, night came and she was still alone. She supposed she was being punished by not being fed, but she hardly cared. Easing open her door, she saw that the corridor outside was clear. She strapped on her sword, pulled her cap over her long hair, and became Renald once more.

Her biggest fear as she moved through the torch-lit corridors was that her father had alerted everyone to her disguise. But she was counting on the fact that her father was too ashamed of what she'd done to spread the story—and that the others wouldn't want to tell anyone a tale in which they had all been beaten by a mere girl.

It seemed as though her hopes were correct. She passed a couple of servants and three soldiers on her way to the armory, and none of them so much as gave her a second glance. When she reached her destination, she was relieved to see that the door was locked and nobody was on duty. With a grin, she fished from her left boot the duplicate key she'd "borrowed" from Borigen a few weeks earlier. He'd always refused to allow her to try the dangerous weapons, like pikes and spears, and she'd been intending to do so once she had a chance. Instead, the stolen key had a better use.

Slipping in to the armory, she found a longbow and a quiver of arrows, which she slung across her back. She then took a water skin and a pouch of dried meat. With those, she'd be able to last a week on foot. She knew that she was skilled enough to cover her tracks and that if she were gone a week, she'd be gone forever. And good riddance to the lot of them. Except Borigen, of course, who was the only friend she'd ever known.

Helaine slipped out of the armory, locked it, and tossed the key into a crack in the paving stones. Now all she had to do was to escape through one of the passageways and out a low-lying window using a length of rope she'd taken from the armory. Then no one could catch her.

The Shadows hovered eagerly over the dark castle, tasting another imminent victory. The girl was on her way to meet her fate. Soon, soon, the second phase of their mission would be complete.

They began to move downward, drifting eagerly toward a group of men waiting in the shadows of the castle's corridors. There were six of them, all creeping carefully through the darkness, all burly and armed, though none had their weapons drawn.

"I don't like this much," one of them muttered. "I know we are here to stop the marriage—and the alliance between Votrin and Peverel. But making war on women isn't my idea of a soldier's job."

"Quiet!" hissed his closest companion. "You have your orders. And we're not making war on women.

We're simply to capture and hold Lord Votrin's daughter until he comes to his senses. You know very well that if he and Peverel are allied, then neither of our lords will be able to stand against them."

"It's still dirty work, unfit for a soldier," the first man grumbled. But he didn't hold back.

The Shadows slid down into the castle's corridors, and each of them took over the mind of a soldier. It was the work of an instant, slipping into their impressionable minds and just making a few small suggestions . . .

Eyes now black because of the Shadows, the six men paused, drew their swords, and changed direction slightly. All at once, as if they only had one mind . . .

Renald rounded the bend of a corridor, finally away from all prying eyes as she hurried toward the closest window. She could hang the rope from a metal torch holder set in the wall, and then use it to climb down to the ground. She unwound the rope, and was about to tie it to the post when a strange itching in the back of her mind made her turn around.

There were six men in the corridor, quietly approaching her, swords drawn and ready to use. She recognized their shields as those of an enemy kingdom. The men's intentions were quite clear.

Renald dropped the rope and drew her own sword, prepared to meet the silent attack. She was lucky the corridor was only wide enough for two of them to stand abreast, and even then the closeness of the walls would hamper their ability to swing their swords. She, on the other hand, had plenty of range.

There were two conflicting emotions warring within her. There was an icy touch of fear in her throat as she watched the six assassins approaching her. She had never fought for her life before. All of her swordplay until now had been practice only. But drowning out that fear was a feeling of exhilaration, that this was what she had been born for, not needlework—or marriage. This was what made her blood sing.

The first two soldiers attacked, leaving her no more time to think.

She parried one blade and twisted to avoid the second. There was not time to counterattack, because each of the men moved fluidly, as though this were an everyday thing for him to do. Perhaps it was. At any rate, though Renald defended herself with all of her skill, she could not break through their swords to attack them in turn.

The other four men just held back, silent, their dark eyes watching emotionlessly, ready to step in if either of the first attackers fell. Renald started to get worried. She was keeping her attackers at bay, but she was bound to tire first. And when she did, they would have her. She briefly considered calling for help, but there wasn't much point. She'd deliberately chosen this spot because nobody normally came here. And if someone did hear and come to her help, then she'd be captured by her father's men and forced to go through with her wedding.

She'd sooner be dead. So she, too, fought in silence, losing ground step-by-step as the men battled hard. Sweat was starting to trickle down her face and her back, and she could feel her muscles beginning to tire. Soon, she was going to make a mistake, and one of those blades would cut into her. That would be the start of her death. Still she fought on, refusing to give in.

And then came a sound she had never heard before. It was a low, feral growl, too loud for any of the castle cats to have made. There was a flicker of shadows from behind Renald, and then something leaped over her head toward the first two soldiers.

Renald threw herself backward, but the creature hadn't aimed for her. As it passed over her head, Renald saw that it was some kind of leopard—orange-tan fur with dark blotches, burning eyes, and fangs and claws of iron.

As it came down upon the two startled soldiers, it began to change, its form flowing from that of a huge cat into that of a cat-woman. But the woman retained her fur coating and her claws, which shredded into the two soldiers as she batted aside their swords. There was a spray of blood, and at last the two men made a sound—dark, dreadful screams, as they fell backward.

The leopard woman whirled to face Renald. "Come," she hissed, her voice silky and urgent, her teeth pointed and dangerous. "We must leave now!"

"Who . . . ?" began Renald, shaken and uncertain. "What are you?"

"I am Rahn," the leopard-woman replied impatiently. "And if you want to live, come with me."

The other four soldiers leaped over the fallen bodies of their comrades, and Renald understood the urgency of Rahn's command. With a nod, she turned and fled after the creature.

The four soldiers chased their two targets down the corridor and around the bend.

Only to see a blank wall, with no other way to exit.

Puzzled, they stopped and stared uncertainly at the heavy stone walls. What could have happened to their victims?

The Shadows, well pleased with their work, coalesced in the air above the thoroughly confused men. The four living soldiers couldn't understand why they had tried to kill a young boy when they had been sent to kidnap a girl from the castle. And they certainly couldn't understand what had happened to their targets.

But the Shadows knew. They knew exactly what had happened to Renald.

She had become their second victim . . . and it was time for them to find their third and final target. Time to slip beyond this world, to one called Calomir. A very different world, where people lived inside houses that served as wombs—feeding them, tending them, and entertaining them. A world where nobody ever had to leave home and would never think of doing so.

But where one person must, in order to become their final victim . . .

3

Pixel was bored. It was a feeling he had grown to know only too well over the past year. He should have been very happy, he knew. Or, at the very least, content. Everyone else he knew was. Then again, he couldn't be certain that anyone else he knew was even real.

That was the problem with Virtual Reality—after a while, it became simple Reality, and he had problems telling where it began and ended.

"How can you be bored?" Digit had asked him. "There's no limit to what you can do here." At the time, they were standing on the bed of some ancient sea, watching a plesiosaurus romp and hunt above them. Strange, armor-plated fish swam past them.

"Yeah," Byte had added, wrinkling her nose.

"Hey, if you don't like this place, we could always go somewhere else. Maybe out to the asteroid belt?"

"It's not this place," Pixel had told them. Digit was his best friend, and Byte his second best. "It's everything." He tried again. "I don't even know if *you're* both real."

Byte shrugged. "So what? We don't know if you're real, either. What difference does it make as long as we have fun?"

"Fun isn't enough," Pixel had replied. He waved his hands around the seabed, watching horseshoe crabs scuttling away. "This doesn't exist. In fact, it may never have existed. It's just a computer generation."

"Yeah, but a way cool one," Digit answered. "What's gotten into you, Pixel? You're usually so much fun."

"I don't really know," he had to admit. "It's just that this has all started to feel so . . . so . . . insufficient." He was grasping at thoughts to try to explain what he meant. "I've been having bad dreams lately," he confessed.

"They'll pass," Byte commented. "Don't let them worry you."

"It's always the same dream," he persisted. "I'm in this really weird place, flickering red. I see these stones of color dangling in a sphere. I see this portrait—it shimmers. It's a picture of a lady—I know that—but whenever I move to take a closer look, I wake up."

"Sounds neat," Byte replied. "Hey, maybe we can get the computer to make up a world like that for us to play in."

"It's not made-up," Pixel said stubbornly. "I get the impression that it's somehow real, somehow important."

"How can it be?" asked Digit. "It's just a dumb dream."

Pixel felt angry. "So is this place, if you think about it," he told them both. "It's not real."

"I wouldn't want it to be," Byte replied with a shudder. "We'd get killed if we were really here. That's why this way is so much better."

"No," Pixel answered. "No, it isn't. It's just a way to escape. And I don't think I want to escape right now."

He moved his right hand, gesturing the command sequence. Just above his head, the menu bar appeared. He tapped at the Exit sign, and then everything went dark. A final trail of words appeared before him: "User Pixel signing off . . . Shalar Domain account closing."

Shalar Domain was his real name, but his online name, Pixel, was what he used the most. He'd almost forgotten the name he'd been born with.

And then he was back in his room, removing his helmet, feeling very dissatisfied, but not knowing why. If Virtual Reality was good enough for his friends, why wasn't it good enough for him?

Pixel rose to his feet from his couch and called out to the House, "Strawberry shake, cold."

A moment later, a small 'bot wheeled out from the kitchen, holding the shake on a tray for him. He sipped it, thoughtfully looking about his room. There was the bed in one corner, and the VR equipment that took up most of the rest of the space. His closet door was hidden in the wall, but the rest of his room was . . . well, bare, he realized. It could belong to anyone. There was nothing in it that marked it as his specifically.

But why bother decorating it when you spent all day in Virtual Reality, where you could be surrounded by anything at all? Pixel realized that he knew next to nothing about real reality.

He couldn't ever remember being anywhere real, except in this house. He knew from his VR travels that many houses were great, elaborate places, some of them built centuries ago by master craftsmen. His house, however, consisted of his room, his parents' room, the bathroom, and the kitchen. Plus the robots' room, of course, where the 'bots waited until needed. And all of the rooms were as bare as this one, except maybe the kitchen. He hadn't been inside there for maybe four years, and he vaguely remembered that it had some cooking equipment in there for the robots to work. And presumably food, of course.

He didn't even know where the food came from, or how it got here. Oh, he could check on it with his computer, of course, but it had never occurred to him before to even wonder about it.

So why was it occurring to him now?

It was that dream, of course. The recurring one. For some reason, it had seemed so real, more real than VR, even though he knew it wasn't. It had given him a taste of reality and awakened a hunger inside him that he never knew existed before.

He finished the shake and put the glass down on the floor. A waiting 'bot scurried in to pick it up and take it away. To be cleaned, he assumed, though it might just as easily throw it in the garbage. He had never wondered what happened to anything he'd finished using. Clothes, for example, he just tossed on the floor when he went to bed. They were gone when he awoke, and he just picked fresh ones from his closet. Were his clothes washed and then replaced in his closet by the House? Or were they thrown out, and fresh ones added when he needed them?

He had no idea. Frowning, Pixel realized that he knew virtually nothing about anything but Virtual Reality. The thought brought a bitter laugh to him. Well, that had gone on for long enough. He was going to do something drastic.

He was going to search for reality.

Uh . . .

"House," he called, "is there any way out of here?"

"Your bedroom door," the voice of the House answered pleasantly. It was neither male nor female, and gentle, soothing.

"Not that," he snorted. "I mean out of the House."

"Out?" asked the House. Computers can't sound surprised, but this one did seem a little . . . puzzled. "I do not understand."

"Because I want to go *out*," Pixel said stubbornly. "Come on, there has to be some way out, doesn't there?"

"Yes," agreed the House. "There is a door. But I would caution you against going through it."

"I don't care what *you'd* do," Pixel said, leaving his room. "*I* want to do it, and you must obey my orders. Where is the door?"

"It is in the kitchen," the House replied. "But I would strongly advise you not to use it."

"Advise away," Pixel muttered. "See if I care." He'd made up his mind, and no dumb House was going to talk him out of it. He entered the kitchen, and was pleased to see that he had been right. There was a sink and a hydrosquall here. Plus a door that presumably led to the pantry. "Okay, where's the door to the outside?" he demanded.

There was a slight pause, as if the House were thinking of disobeying him. Then a thin line appeared in the far, blank wall. The line widened to a gap.

"Shalar," the House said, using his real name for the first time in Pixel's memory, "do not leave the premises. You do not know what is out there."

"No," agreed Pixel, walking slowly toward the door. "I don't. That's why I have to go and find out." He stepped out of the House and into reality.

It was slightly colder than the House, he discovered, and the air moved a lot faster than the gentle breeze of the air-conditioning. He didn't care.

"I shall send a 'bot with you to help," the voice of the House said from inside the kitchen.

"No," said Pixel firmly. "I'm going alone. I don't need looking after. Now, close the door."

Again there was that reluctant pause, but the House had no choice. It had to obey, and the door slid silently shut.

Pixel grinned to himself. He was outside, in the real world!

He marched away from the door toward the road the House stood on. Turning, he looked back at it. He couldn't remember ever being outside of it before, and he saw that it was a completely featureless box shape, about twenty feet wide, thirty long, and ten high. There were no windows or visible doors and no architectural embellishments like the older houses in VR had. Well, since nobody ever saw the outside, why bother?

Pixel looked around. As far as he could see, there were other featureless, box-shaped houses just like his.

Reality, in fact, looked very dull.

He didn't care. There had to be something other than this, and he would find it. He was going to have a real adventure, not one dreamed up by some computer or programmer. It would be his, and his alone.

He set off down the deserted street, humming to himself and staring all around, hoping to see something.

Pixel continued walking for about an hour, until his feet were getting tired. Then he sat down on the nearest lawn to rest and consider what he'd discovered about reality so far. It wasn't much. Reality consisted of a lot of boxes on lawns. And clouds in the sky. And a breeze that felt nice and refreshing.

Pixel was starting to get a little hungry and thirsty. "House," he called, and then stopped, with a smile. He wasn't in the house, was he? How could it hear him and bring him anything?

And then he started to worry.

He'd better go back again, he supposed. And then another realization came to him.

He didn't know where the House was. He'd been walking for a while and taken several different roads at random. And all of the houses looked absolutely alike, with nothing to distinguish his house from the rest. In VR, he had never really been lost.

Pixel was really getting unsettled now. He glanced at the closest house to him. There were no numbers or addresses on them. Then how did delivery trucks get to them? He winced. They were computer guided, of course, and he wasn't.

He walked slowly up to the outside of the house and stared at it closely. Nothing at all, save a blank wall. Still, maybe he could get some help here. "House?" he called, gently. He assumed that the computer here was like the one back home.

"Unknown user," the House replied. "Leave immediately."

"Please," Pixel begged, "I need help. I'm lost and I don't know where my House is."

"Unknown user," the House responded. "Police will be notified."

Pixel swallowed. "But I just want help!"

"Police will be notified," the House repeated.

Defeated, Pixel turned and walked away from the house. When he looked in one direction, something inside of him seemed to be convinced that it was the right way to go. Maybe he was just imagining it, but what difference could it make? Any direction could be right or wrong. He went the way he felt he should.

And then he jumped, as he realized that there was somebody suddenly walking beside him. Someone who hadn't been there a second earlier. Pixel stared at him in astonishment. He was tall and shadowy, dressed completely in black. He grinned down at Pixel and winked.

"Where did you come from?" Pixel asked in surprise.

It's not important where I'm from,
But for your aid is why I've come.

The man answered in a singsong kind of rhyme.

"To help me?" Pixel said eagerly. "You can guide me home?"

That way, I fear, is closed to you.
But I will lead you someplace new.

The man gestured ahead, the way they were walking.

"I don't understand you," Pixel admitted. "Why can't I go home? Where are you leading me?"

Call me Relcoa; I'm your guide.
When danger nears, I'm by your side.
Seek out two more, Renald and Score.
You'll all find what you're searching for.

"What do you mean?" Pixel asked. He was chilled to notice Relcoa didn't have a shadow.

An emergency exists, it's true,
And danger's on its way to you.
Two friends exist whom you must find,
For they are both of your own kind.

Pixel suddenly realized that the afternoon was drawing to a close. A glorious red sunset was tingeing the sky. That meant it would soon be dark, and he had nowhere to stay. He was still hungry and thirsty, and was getting very tired. And there didn't seem to be any change in the monotony of the houses.

Maybe he should go to another house and have it call the police? They'd probably be able to help him. After all, he wasn't a criminal or anything.

And then he saw an end to the houses. There was a wall across the street, and he realized that is was taller than the houses and stretched along some kind of ridge. Glad to see some sort of change, he ran toward it. He realized abruptly that Relcoa had somehow vanished again. Well, if he were just a projection, that was hardly surprising.

Reaching the wall, Pixel saw that it led off downward, following the line of the ridge. To his right, he could see over the top. Beyond the wall was a grayish area, with long, wooden buildings containing lots and lots of people—men, women, and children. They were all dressed in drab gray clothes and looked exhausted and dispirited.

Standing over them were police officers, equipped with large machine guns.

Suddenly the idea of getting help from the police seemed pretty undesirable. They might think he was one of those prisoners who had escaped . . . But who were those people, and what were they doing there?

Relcoa suddenly walked up to join him again. He must have realized what Pixel was wondering, because he said,

These workers toil their lives away
To make the things you want each day.

With a shock, Pixel understood what the stranger meant. The things that he ordered from the House were made by these slaves in the prison camp. They—and probably millions more like them—had to work all day to allow people like Pixel and his family to live carefree lives, getting whatever they wanted without a thought.

He turned away from the wall and started to run. He didn't care where; he just wanted to get away from the awful sight. He couldn't live with the knowledge that all of his things were bought at the expense of so many people living miserable lives.

Pixel heard the sound of a dog barking. He glanced up, puzzled. This was the first sound he'd heard all the time he'd been outside, apart from sighing of the wind. The first bark was answered by a chorus of more dogs. They seemed to be moving—heading in his direction, in fact. Pets? He'd never owned a pet, of course. Too much trouble to look after, and unnecessary when, in Virtual Reality, you could have any animal you liked, and it didn't need to be fed or have its litter box scooped, and it never, ever died on you.

He imagined that most people would feel that way. So what were these dogs, then?

Worry gnawed at his mind. And then he had the answer. A pack of about thirty lean, hungry-looking dogs came from behind one of the houses. They stared at him and began to move forward. They were of all shapes and sizes, but they all looked nasty, and they all had peculiar eyes—completely black. Now they had stopped their barking and seemed intent on coming after him.

Pixel realized then what they were. They were dogs that had once been pets, but had then been allowed to run wild. Most of them would have died out, but some, tougher than others, would have survived on any food they could scavenge.

Or hunt . . .

And he was outside, alone and unarmed.

Slowly, grimly, they padded forward, mouths open and drooling.

Pixel turned and ran. Instantly, he heard the sound of the dogs' paws on the road behind him as they, too, started to run. Pixel was terrified, knowing he couldn't escape them. He'd seen a VR once in which a pack of wild dogs attacked some kind of deer.

Driven by desperation, Pixel pushed his tired body onward. There was a snap of teeth at his ankle, barely missing his skin.

Then, suddenly, there was an angry cry and a whirl of wings. A shadow passed overhead, elongated in the dying rays of the sun, and Pixel could feel the dogs' uncertainty and their own fear of this new predator. Pixel risked a glance upward, scared that he might be saved from the dogs only to be taken by a different creature.

It was some kind of huge eagle, golden brown in color, that was swooping down. Its talons were outstretched, its beak wide. Pixel thought it was aiming for the dogs, but he wasn't absolutely certain. It was whipping down so fast from the sky that it was almost a blur. Scared, Pixel dived to one side, but stumbled and fell.

The dogs, seeing their chance, leaped toward him.

The eagle had landed, somehow, and was no longer simply a bird. It seemed to be almost man-shaped, though it was still feathered, and its head was beaked. But its claws were long and vicious as it tore into the dogs. It was clearly protecting him for some reason. Pixel managed to stagger back to his feet, wondering what to do now.

The eagle-man threw two dogs into the rest of the pack, whirled, and grabbed hold of Pixel's arm. "We must leave," he growled. "Now. I am Hakar. You must come with me."

"Come where?" asked Pixel, amazed that his rescuer could even speak.

"Away from here."

That sounded good to Pixel. The dogs were starting to close in again. "Okay," he agreed. "But how do we do it?"

"Like this." Hakar concentrated and stretched out a clawed hand. On one finger, Pixel saw a ring with a gemstone in it. There was a flare of light, and then the air in front of them seemed to be torn open, and a jagged hole appeared. It was like some kind of a rip in space, deep black and with a chill to it.

"Through there," the eagle-man urged.

Pixel wasn't so sure this was a good idea. He could see nothing at all in the gap, and he was scared.

"Uh, I don't know," he muttered.

"Would you prefer to be torn apart?" asked Hakar, pointedly.

Screwing up all of his courage, Pixel jumped forward at the black rip in space. He passed through it, into darkness, and heard the eagle-man follow behind.

To . . . where?

As the eagle-man vanished into the gap, it sizzled and closed before any of the dogs could follow. The Shadows emerged from the possessed dogs, leaving the poor animals confused and whining at what they had been subjected to.

The Shadows, elated, rose in the air, leaving Calomir behind them. It was now time for their return home, to inform their Master that the last of the three had been gathered. Everything was going according to plan.

4

Instead of hitting the water as Score had expected—or crashing onto the rocks as he'd feared—Score slammed down rather painfully on grass. Stunned in more ways than one, it took a few minutes before he could force himself up on his hands and knees to see what had happened to him.

One thing was for sure—this place wasn't New York. Or anywhere he'd ever seen featured in *National Geographic*, for that matter.

The grass under him and the trees about him seemed quite normal. Well, they would be if he had been in Washington state, for example, and not in where the East River was supposed to be flowing. The trees were tall and leafy, blocking the hot afternoon sun. They gave the place a kind of let's-go-on-a-picnic feel. Until he looked farther.

The whatever-it-was who had saved his life was hunched down, staring calmly at him. A shiver passed through Score as he examined the whale-man in his turn. The man looked almost normal, if you could ignore his weird skin coloring. He was completely hairless as far as Score could see, and didn't seem to be in any rush to speak.

Behind him, tied to a rope stretched between two trees, were three horses. They looked like the kind of beasts that pulled the carriages in Central Park. The horses were ignoring him, munching on the grass while they waited.

Finally, Score asked, "Where am I?"

The whale-man said simply, "Treen."

Score was more chilled then ever. The words on the strange page: "Treen is the start!" He remembered the message . . . and this was Treen . . . The start of what?

He was on some weird alien planet. Score shook his head. This was way too far out for him to accept just like that. He was confused and needed more information. S'hee seemed to be willing to supply it. Score was scared and disturbed, but there was at least one positive thing about this whole situation. He was away from New York. But—where had he come to? And why?

"What kind of person are you?" he asked S'hee.

"I am not a person," S'hee answered with dignity. "I am a Bestial."

"A what?"

S'hee stared at him, puzzled, and then sighed. "So, it is true—there are no Bestials on your world?"

"Trust me, there's nothing like you on my world." Score stared at him. "How do you do that morphing stuff?"

"Morphing? You mean changing between states?" He shrugged. "How do you breathe? I simply do it."

"Cool." Score managed to sit up now. "You're like some kind of offbeat werewolf, then?"

"Werewolf?" S'hee looked puzzled. "Some of my kindred are wolflings, yes. I am a whalebeing myself. We await others, who are also different."

"We do?" Score looked around. "Why?"

"It is my task," S'hee answered. Then, cocking his head, he added, "Another comes."

Score couldn't hear or see anything, but maybe this Bestial had keener senses than he had.

A dark tear in space appeared about ten feet away from him. It was just like the one he and S'hee had fallen into. So this whole thing wasn't just for him.

There would be another person coming here. What was going on?

As he stared at the tear, two figures hurled themselves through. Then the gap simply folded in on itself and vanished again. Score rose to his feet, wondering if this was going to be another attack, but S'hee merely nodded at one of the newcomers without concern. It probably meant it was okay, then. If he could trust the Bestials.

The first of the new arrival was obviously another Bestial. Judging from her fur and her feline features, she was some kind of leopard-woman. She was furred all over, and kind of cute—if you were into fangs and claws.

The other person was apparently a boy of about the same age as Score. He looked like he'd just stepped right out of a King Arthur movie, though. He wore what looked like rough battle clothing and carried a sword and a bow and arrows. He turned dark eyes on S'hee, and then Score.

"Where am I?" he finally asked.

"Treen," Score told him. "That's the name of this planet. I'm Score." He held out his hand.

The other boy stared at him for a moment, as if sizing him up, and then extended his own hand. "I am Hel— Renald," he offered. "I am on another world?"

Good question, Score thought. "We both are," Score told him. "At least, I think we are. Maybe we're both dead, and this is the afterlife." He wrinkled his nose. "Though it smells too much like horses for my idea of heaven. Or maybe I'm just going crazy, and none of this is really happening. I could have hit my head pretty hard." He nodded at where the leopard-woman had crouched to wait with S'hee. "They're something called Bestials," he added. "They don't have them on my world. They're half man—or woman—and half animal. They can change back and forth. It's pretty wild."

"So I observed," Renald said dryly. His eyes took in the horses, and he finally showed a little enthusiasm.

"They are fine animals. I assume we are waiting for a third person, from their number."

Score shrugged. "I guess. S'hee there isn't exactly talkative."

"Nor is Rahn," admitted Renald. He stepped forward. "When do we get some explanations?" he demanded, somewhat arrogantly. He was obviously used to taking charge.

"When you reach Aranak," Rahn answered. "He will explain everything to you."

"Why don't you?" asked Renald aggressively.

"Because I do not know everything."

"You knew I was in trouble," Renald pointed out.

"It was Aranak who told me you were in trouble." Rahn looked bored with the conversation.

Score glanced around. This place had obviously been prepared for them. "So how come he isn't here?" he wondered aloud. Was this some kind of trap? And how did his mother—or whoever had written the strange letter—know the name of this place? Score felt better knowing he had it with him still, in his wallet. As soon as he could do so without being observed, he was going to check the page and see if he could figure out what it meant.

S'hee shrugged. "I'm sure Aranak will tell you what he wants you to know when you meet him."

"I think you know more than you're telling us," said Renald stubbornly.

"Let it rest," Score advised. "Either they don't know, or they won't tell."

Renald glared at him impatiently. "Do you have any idea why we are here? Or where *here* really is?"

"Not a clue," Score admitted. "I wish I did. This is really unsettling. I'm not sure I like it here. And I am sure I really don't want to be here. I'd sooner take my chances back in New York. At least I know that turf." He gestured at the trees. "This place scares me."

"The last one comes!" announced Rahn, rising to her feet and gesturing.

Again, there was a plucking at the air as the dark tear slashed into being. Once more, two figures fell to Treen.

The first was a sort of eagle man. He nodded to his two waiting companions and drew the final person in the group—a small, nervous-looking kid with pale-blue skin and pointed ears. Alien, Score decided, but manageable.

"Hi," Score greeted him. "I'm Score, this," he gestured to his companion, "is Renald, and this planet is called Treen. Those guys," he added, gesturing to the animal-beings, "are called Bestials. With me so far?"

"I think so," the new kid said, frowning. "Is this really another planet?" He looked around in awe. "It's much nicer than mine."

"I think it is," Score answered, trying to sound casual. In fact, his stomach was struggling to remain calm.

"Uh, my name's Pixel." The newcomer shook Score's hand, then Renald's.

"It is time to move," S'hee informed them. "We have a journey to make. Mount your horses."

"How do you do that?" asked Score. "I'm a city kid, myself."

"Like this," Renald answered scornfully. He untied a white steed from the line, gripped the reins, and placed his left foot in the stirrup. He then swung up and into the saddle. "It's quite simple."

"Yeah, right," muttered Score. He eyed the other two horses with suspicion, then picked a palomino that seemed to be the smaller and more placid of the two. Renald's horse was the fieriest, snorting and whuffing. Score wanted one that would just plod. He untied the animal, then grabbed the reins. He managed to get into the saddle on the third attempt—

ignoring Renald's chuckles at his efforts. "Hey, that wasn't too bad," he admitted, clutching the reins for dear life and sitting bolt upright in the saddle, terrified in case the animal took off or threw him or something. "Uh, they don't buck or anything, do they?"

Renald snorted. "These are trained animals," he replied. "They will not harm you . . . intentionally." He turned his amused eyes on Pixel, who had also finally managed to get into his saddle on the black-and-white paint horse. "We shall have to travel slowly, I imagine, so you don't fall out of your seats."

"Good idea," Score agreed, not bothered by Renald's look of contempt. "Next time, we travel by subway, though. I'd love to see how you do catching an E train."

"I have no idea what you are talking about," Renald said.

"My point exactly," Score told him. "It's easy for you to be smug right now, since you're the only one who's been on a horse before. But that doesn't make you any better than us."

Renald stared at him in contempt. "My father is Lord Votrin," he snapped. "I am a high-born noble. I am also a warrior. *That* makes me better than you." He eyed Score's battered clothing. "A lowly street rat and a thief by the look of you."

"Yeah," agreed Score with a grin. "But a darned good thief, if you don't mind, your majesty."

With a final snort, Renald turned away from him to face S'hee. The Bestials started off at a trot. Score stared down at his horse. "Go," he suggested. How were you supposed to start these things? The only command he knew for around horses was "whoa!" and that was to stop them. Pixel looked equally lost.

Renald sighed. "Use your knees," he ordered. "Press them once inward, and then give a flick of your reins." He demonstrated, and his steed started moving after the departing Bestials.

Doing as he had been told, Score was quite amazed when his horse actually started to amble along behind Renald's. Pixel managed to fall in line behind him, and they were off to see this Aranak, whoever he was. Hopefully, they would be able to get some answers from him.

It was still nothing much but woods. Quite pretty, really, and a lot different from the Bowery. But a guy could take only so many trees, bushes, and flowers before they all started looking alike. This was like a long trip through a park and not exactly what he would have expected to find on some alien planet. Where were the fabulous cities or spaceship docks or ravenous monsters? Where were the alien beings? Well, maybe the Bestials counted as aliens, but they seemed . . . well, somehow not quite as alien as he'd expected. He wondered how far they had to go and considered asking S'hee. But if the Bestial had wanted them to know, surely he'd have mentioned it. With an inward shrug, Score decided to just wait and see.

He just wished some of this would start making sense. The letter was burning a hole in his pocket, and he desperately wanted to read it and try to figure it out. It had to be something—advice, a warning, a map maybe—something to clue him in, to give him an edge. Score desperately needed an edge. He knew he'd never be able to survive without an advantage of some kind. And, underlying everything, there was the desperate fear that this was some kind of complicated trap.

"I'm hungry," complained Pixel. "And thirsty."

Score realized that he was, too. He glanced at the sky. It seemed to be about midmorning here. Yesterday seemed like a long time ago. "Yeah," he agreed. "A burger and a soda would be great about now. Except I don't see any take-outs." There was nothing at all in sight to eat or drink.

Renald sighed heavily. "Did you bring anything with you?"

"Just my attitude," Score answered. "I wasn't exactly expecting to be hustled onto another planet, you know, even if you were."

Without another word, Renald unslung the pouch and water skin from his shoulders and passed them over to Pixel. The skinny boy almost fell off his horse reaching for them. That made Renald raise his eyebrows again. "Take some, then pass it along to Score. And you," he added to Score, "back to me. I don't know how long that will have to last us."

"Yes, sire," said Score, mockingly. He waited until Pixel had drunk and taken a long strip of meat from the pouch before helping himself. He passed the bags back to Renald, noticing that the other boy also had a drink and then took some food. Score bit into the meat. It was tough and strong-tasting. "What is this stuff?"

"Smoked venison," Renald answered. "It's dried so it lasts longer."

It took Score a considerable amount of biting and chewing to get some into his mouth. "Yeah. It lasts longer because it's almost impossible to eat."

"Would you like to give it back?" asked Renald.

"Uh, no. It's okay."

Renald shrugged, and they continued on their way in silence. Once more, they rode through a dense forest. The Bestials didn't seem to be tiring, despite the fact that they had been trotting for several hours. Score looked at the side of the road—nothing but stones and sticks. Except for one strange rock—an eerie symbol had been painted on it, a red triangle, crossed out by an X. Score wondered what it meant.

"Do we have much farther to go?" Renald called to S'hee. It was the leopard-woman, Rahn, who answered, though.

"Possibly two more hours. We must avoid the village."

"Why do we have to avoid it?" asked Pixel. "Couldn't we stop there?"

Rahn laughed derisively. "Only if you wish to die there, child."

Renald frowned. "They would kill us for no reason?"

"They believe they have reason," Rahn answered, dropping back slightly to converse with the three riders as she ran. "They hate all Bestials and would kill us for being what we are. And they hate all magic-users and would kill you for being that."

"Magic-users?" asked Pixel, echoing the confusion that Score felt. "But we're not magic-users. I don't even believe in magic."

"What you *believe* in is unimportant," the woman laughed, showing her fangs. "Magic *is*. And you must all be magic-users, otherwise you could not have come through the Gateways."

Pixel's eyes narrowed. "The Gateways are the gap in space we went through," he said slowly, obviously catching her meaning. "And if only magic-users can travel through them, then we must be magicians. And so must you."

"I?" Rahn snorted in disgust. "Not I! No Bestial can use magic, because magic makes us what we are. Since we are magical, we cannot therefore bend magic to our wills. But we can move through the Gateways. Of humans, only magic-users can traverse the Gateways. Therefore, you must be magic-users."

Score remembered the changed hundred-dollar bills in his pocket. "Maybe we are," he said slowly. "I can do some things," he informed the others. "Like sleight of hand." He still had a bit of the tough venison in his hand, and gave a grin. "Like this," he suggested. Closing his eyes, he tried to focus on the tough meat, picturing instead a nice, juicy burger . . .

And then he looked at his hand, which suddenly had a hot meat patty in it. "Ow!" But he kept his grip on it, and managed to bite some off. "I should have remembered the bun, too," he grumbled.

"That's incredible," Pixel said, staring at Score. "How do you do that?"

"You heard the lady," Score answered. "Magic." He didn't want to admit to the others how spooked he was to discover he could do that trick. This place was getting weirder by the minute.

Renald nodded tensely. "I, apparently, can foresee attacks," he offered. "What is your ability?"

"I'm not sure," Pixel shrugged.

Score scanned the trees. "So, these villagers don't like people like us?"

"No," agreed Rahn. She alone hadn't been amazed at what Score had done. Maybe she saw stuff like that all day. "They would kill you to prevent you from ruling them."

"Ruling them?" Score said. "Why would we want to do that?"

Rahn shrugged. "I don't know. Humans are like that. And the magicians are the ones who rule. They have the power to force others to obey them. Such is Aranak, the wizard."

"You mean he's in charge here?" asked Pixel. "He's a big magician? Then why haven't the villagers killed him?"

"They would like to," Rahn admitted. "But his power is too great for them, and they cannot. He will be able to keep you safe, too, once we reach his tower." She paused. "But he is not exactly in charge, save of this immediate world. There are others whom he, too, must obey, because they have greater power than he possesses."

Renald suddenly held up a hand, taking command instantly. "Trouble! I feel it coming."

The Bestial didn't question him. Spinning, Rahn scanned the trees and bushes.

At that moment, several heavily armed men stepped out into the open, swords drawn and ready for use.

Renald had been perfectly correct: trouble.

5

Renald smiled to herself as she saw the way the men waited for them. There were only a dozen of them, all armed only with swords and knives. From the look of them, they weren't too accustomed to holding them, either. This was a really pathetic ambush.

"Stand aside," she said, loudly and commandingly. It didn't work, though several of the men shuffled their feet uncertainly.

"Filthy magic-user," said their leader, a tall man with shaggy, untidy black hair. He spat on the ground. "Keeps company with Bestials, too. It figures." He shook his head in disgust. "You can't trust Bestials, boy. They'll turn on you whenever they get a chance."

Renald had simply assumed command of the group. It was logical. Neither Score nor Pixel could handle a weapon. The Bestials, though leading them, seemed to be uncertain what to do at this moment. Rahn stood staring at the men, her fangs bared, her claws ready to strike. S'hee simply scowled. It was impossible to read Hakar's features, which were too different because of his beak.

"To get to any of my companions," Renald stated clearly, "you will have to go through me. And none of you has that kind of skill." Renald wasn't boasting, simply stating facts. It would be better if she could just scare off the villagers rather than have to fight—and perhaps kill—some of them.

"But even you can't take on all of us at once, child," their leader said.

"We have no quarrel with you," Renald said. "Let us pass, and no more need be said."

"You'll only get past us over our dead bodies," the man growled back.

"It's your choice," Renald answered with a bluffing sigh. She started to get off her horse.

Score grabbed her arm. "What do you think you're doing?" he asked. "Why don't we just ride these horses right through them?"

Renald scowled. "That would be the action of a coward, not a warrior."

"Well, I am not a warrior," Score protested. "You may know what to do with that overgrown steak knife of yours, but Pixel and I aren't used to sword fights."

"I understand that," agreed Renald patiently. "But I am, and will deal with it my way."

"Who made you boss?" Score demanded.

"I am the offspring of a Lord of Ordin," Renald explained. "Plus, as you pointed out, I am the only warrior here."

Pixel moved slightly closer. "Wait a minute," he said. "There's something not right about this."

"What do you mean?" asked Renald.

"They're just waiting for you to go to them," Pixel pointed out.

"That is what warriors do," Renald explained.

"But they're not warriors," Pixel explained. "They're villagers who just want to massacre us for being what we are. Why didn't they just attack us from ambush, instead of warning us?" Renald began to see his point. "Because there are more on the way, and this group is just trying to delay us. That's why they're waiting, not attacking."

Renald nodded grimly, realizing that Pixel was correct. "And the next group will likely have archers," she agreed. "That way, they can cut us down without having to get too close to us." She thought for a moment. "That changes matters." To the Bestials, she called, "Hakar! Can you fly to freedom?"

"Of course!" the eagle-man answered. "But I cannot leave you when you need me."

"Go to Aranak," Renald said. "Tell him of this ambush." She said it loudly enough for the villagers to hear. "Tell him we need his aid."

Hakar gave an abrupt nod, seeing the wisdom of the request. He leaped upward, and his body flowed, becoming that of a giant eagle again. With great wings beating, he rose into the sky and swiftly vanished.

Renald grinned at the unsettled villagers. "As soon as he reaches Aranak, you'll be in trouble," she pointed out. "So let us through."

Their leader shook his head. "By that time, you'll all be dead." He gestured with his sword. "Come on, men!"

The main thing now was to get away before reinforcements arrived. Her plans changed, Renald spurred on her horse, drew her sword, and gave a battle cry as she rode toward the villagers.

The weak villagers were intimidated by the charge of the warhorse. Several of them simply dived aside. Only three stood their ground, including their leader. He held his sword out, ready to go for the horse. It was a smart move, because Renald could not endanger her steed.

At the last instant before impact, she whirled the animal to the left and struck out with her own sword. The blow was hard and sent the other man reeling back from the impact. The second man thrust for her, but he had to strike upward in an attempt to get at her, and she brought her own blade in the way to intercept and turn aside the blow. For good measure, she kicked out at him, catching him in the chest and sending him sprawling. The third man, seeing his comrades both down, hesitated. In that moment of weakness, Renald hit him with the side of her blade instead of the edge. The blow sent the man stumbling, his head addled.

Three down in the first moment . . .

Rahn had leaped forward with Renald, and had savagely clawed one man aside. He lay on the ground, howling and bleeding. A second held Rahn at bay with his sword dancing, but there was fear in his eyes, and the leopard-woman could obviously sense it. S'hee now lumbered up, unarmed, but still quite formidable. One attacker went for him, and S'hee simply grabbed the man's arm, shook him until his weapon fell, and then tossed him aside like a discarded chicken bone. Stooping, S'hee snatched up the sword and was also armed.

Score and Pixel had managed to get their horses moving in the right direction, but would be useless in this fight. They could barely control their mounts on a gentle ride, let alone in battle. "Keep going!" Renald called to them. "We'll catch up." Pixel nodded tightly, and the two of them set off.

With half of their number down in the first seconds of the fight, the villagers retreated. Those fallen were the bravest among them, and now only the fearful were left.

Renald gave her war cry again and whirled her sword as she advanced on her horse at the cluster of remaining men. They scattered and fled, as she'd expected.

This was hardly even a scrap, let alone a battle. It was beneath her dignity to chase the cowards.

Then she saw the reinforcements that Pixel had predicted. They were heading through the trees, and all held longbows, several with arrows ready. They were still out of range, but it would not be wise to wait around.

"Move!" she ordered the Bestials.

The beast-man and -woman nodded and whirled to follow where Pixel and Score were leading. Renald howled again and urged her own horse after the others. In moments, she was level with them. They would be out of trouble any second.

Score looked back at her. She saw unacknowledged fear in his eyes—which changed to shock. "Look out!" he yelled, gesturing.

At that second, Renald's own magical alarm went off, wrenching hard at her stomach. She glanced back to see that the archers had all fired. Most arrows would go wide at this range. But not all. Two arrows whipped down toward her. She started to veer aside, knowing that she could avoid one, but the other . . .

Score reached out his clenched fist, muttering to himself, and then he closed his eyes and twisted his fist.

The arrow was upon her. For a second, Renald saw her death.

Only to be hit by a spray of rose petals instead.

Score's talent was at work again, this time saving her life.

"Rose petals?" she turned to him, bewildered.

He looked embarrassed. "Sorry. It was the first thing that came into my head. I wasn't even sure I could change the arrow at all. I've only changed things I've been touching before." He grinned, recovering his bravado. "Guess I must be a hot-shot magic-user, eh?"

It didn't come easy for Renald, but she had to say it. "Thank you for saving my life. I may have misjudged you."

Score shrugged off her thanks. "Anytime."

Renald realized that these new companions might take some getting used to. And she didn't want to get used to them. She wanted . . .

In an instant, Renald's thoughts turned strange. Suddenly, she was elsewhere. She seemed to be standing in a room, even though she could still feel she was sitting on a horse. She couldn't make out much of the room, except there was a person standing at a lectern. On the lectern was a book. A single candle cast sufficient light for Renald to see the person's hand slip a page into the book. It was too dark to read what was on the page, but she knew instinctively it was something important. The figure closed the book, and Renald's heart quickened. It was the book that she had been seeing in her dreams. But how had she come here? And where was here? The figure started to turn, to look at her.

A hand was shaking her roughly. "Renald," Score said, puzzled and obviously scared. "Are you okay?"

She was back with the others in the forest again. No, she realized, she had never really left it. She had simply seen somewhere else. Or she was hallucinating. The shock of being on an alien planet might be catching up with her, she knew. She shouldn't place too much belief in these visions . . .

And yet, she knew that it hadn't simply been her mind playing tricks on her.

"I'm fine," she lied, brushing off Score's hand. "Let's ride."

After about fifteen minutes, she reined in her steed and called to Pixel and Score to do the same. "I'm sure we've lost them by now," she said. "There's little need for further hurry." She glanced around. Rahn was still with them, her chest heaving slightly, but S'hee was nowhere to be seen. "Where's your friend?" she asked the leopard-woman. "He made it through, didn't he?"

"Yes," Rahn replied. "He is simply not built for speed, though. He will catch up to us later, I am sure." She gestured ahead. "We are almost at Aranak's tower now."

"And still no sign of any help from the great magician," murmured Pixel.

"He may have other things to do," Rahn replied.

"Yeah, much more important than saving our lives," agreed Score, sarcastically. "Some good magician."

Rahn shrugged. "I did not say he was good," she answered. "You cannot judge magicians by normal standards. And oftentimes they have their own interests at heart."

"I see," Renald said thoughtfully. "Well, since we are close, we'd better press on and allow S'hee to catch up with us when he can." She nodded to Rahn, who led the way again.

There was a sudden cry from the air, and Renald looked up, alert for further trouble. She relaxed when she saw that it was just Hakar returning. The gigantic bird flew down to join them and started to shimmer as it approached the ground, ready to change back into his man form. Then Hakar screamed, not a warning this time but a cry of pain. He landed on a strange purple tree, squawking and shrieking in high-pitched tones. It was difficult to read the birdlike face, but Renald thought Hakar was definitely in pain. After a moment, he launched himself into the air again and flew off.

"What was that all about?" Pixel asked, worried.

"It is the disruption again," Rahn replied with a shrug. "Hakar could not shift shapes. It will clear later."

"Let me guess," Renald growled. "That's something else that Aranak is going to explain, right?"

"Correct." Rahn led the way again.

This was indeed beautiful countryside, and it cheered Renald's heart. It was lush, with plenty of trees and bushes. Her practiced eye saw signs of deer and other animals that would be marvelous hunting. There were grouse and pheasants and other birds. She couldn't help smiling. This was definitely her kind of land.

Score caught her grin. "You like this place?" he asked her.

"It's beautiful," she replied, irritated by his reaction. "Good hunting and fishing. Pleasing to the eye."

"Not my eye," he informed her. "I like sidewalks and skyscrapers myself. I'm not into the wilderness."

She shrugged. "You must lead a very bleak life," she replied.

For once, he looked uncertain. "Yeah," he finally admitted. "It's the pits." He stared around. "If there were a couple of good movie theaters, this place might be halfway decent."

Renald didn't know what to say to this boy. The world he was from had to be a dreadful place if he didn't want to go back. Then again, she was hardly one to talk, since she didn't have any interest in returning to her own world, either. Maybe Pixel felt the same way, but the thin boy was silent as he rode stiffly beside them.

"The tower," announced Rahn, gesturing.

Renald stared at the building ahead of them with interest. She had been expecting a building that was like a castle keep—tall, made of stone, with maybe a moat or ditch about it. She had not expected what she now saw.

The tower rose about a hundred and fifty feet into the air, and it appeared to be carved out of a single, precious stone. Smoky blue light seemed to be curled up inside it. There were neither obvious doors nor windows, nor was there a moat or any sign of defense.

"Yeah," Pixel said. "That looks like a place where a wizard would live. I think it's deliberate," he added thoughtfully. "It's a warning to the villagers. They'd be real cautious about getting near something this fabulous."

"True." Renald saw the logic of it. "But how do we get inside?" She glanced at Rahn.

The Bestial shrugged. "I have finished my task," she announced. "I was to bring you this far. I must return to my home. If the magician wants you inside, he will make a door for you." She held out her arm. "You fight well—for a human."

Renald shook the proffered paw. "And you fight well, too." The Bestial nodded, turned, and sprinted back for the trees.

Score sighed and stared at the tower. "Now what?"

Renald slipped from her saddle. "We'd better walk the rest of the way," she decided. "That will give this Aranak time to see us approaching."

"Wouldn't he use a crystal ball for that?" asked Score, only half sarcastically.

"I don't know what a magician would do," Renald answered simply. "I imagine we shall soon discover the answer." She led the way to the tower, the two boys behind her.

Close up, the crystal tower was even more impressive. She saw that the smoky blueness was not some kind of illusion. There appeared to be vapors writhing inside the walls. To keep people from seeing inside, or for other purposes? She didn't know. There was still no sign of a door, though.

"Should we knock?" asked Score.

"On what?" Pixel wondered.

"The only thing there is," Renald finished. She rapped once with her knuckles on the smoky crystal.

A strange set of symbols appeared on the wall.

"What does that mean?" Score groaned.

"It's a code of some sort," Pixel explained, examining it closely.

"Is it a word?" Renald asked.

Pixel nodded. "I think it's two words," he said. "I think we have to look at it closely. We have to look at it in a different way."

Score, Renald, and Pixel stared at the shapes for a few minutes, constantly on guard. Score was so frustrated that he looked ready to kick the wall down. Only Pixel's calm concentration prevented him from doing so.

After a few minutes, Pixel said, "I've got it."

"You do?" Renald asked.

"Yes," Pixel answered, picking up a stick. "It's reverse lettering. Pretend each letter is trapped in a square. We're seeing the part of the square that isn't filled by a letter."

"So what does it say?" Score wondered, impatiently.

" 'Type command,' " Pixel sighed. "But we don't know what the command is."

"Try 'open,' " Renald suggested.

Pixel picked up the stick and began to trace shapes onto the wall.

Renald watched, amazed, as the letters were absorbed by the crystal wall. There was a second of wrenching inside her body, and then they were no longer standing outside the tower. They were in a bright, airy room. The horses had vanished, and a man had appeared instead. He sat in a huge armchair, cross-legged, sipping from a cup. There was a small table with three other steaming cups on it and more chairs. Around the walls were rows and rows of bookcases, most of them stuffed to overflowing.

The person—obviously Aranak—smiled at them over the rim of his cup. "Do have a seat and some tea," he offered. "You must be parched after your journey here."

"No soda?" asked Score, flopping casually into a chair. "Hey, nevermind." His face tensed a moment, and his thin, greenish tea became a thicker, brownish liquid. "There is now."

Renald took a seat and sipped at the tea. It tasted slightly spiced and delicious. Pixel was the last to sit and try his own drink.

"Well," Aranak said cheerfully. "I'm sure you have lots of questions, so you may as well start asking them. I'll answer the ones I want to, and ignore the rest."

6

Pixel began, "Why didn't you help us?"

Aranak raised an eyebrow. "Well, for two reasons. First of all, I have no obligation to help you. And secondly, I wanted you to understand that this is a dangerous world."

Pixel's eyes narrowed. "And you wanted to see if we could survive. It wasn't a coincidence that those villagers just happened to have ambushed us, was it?"

"No." Aranak took another sip of his tea. "I deliberately told them where to find you."

Pixel looked sharply at the magician. He'd just admitted betraying them and endangering their lives. Was this a man they could trust? Or had they fallen into a trap? They didn't know anything about this magician—or what he had planned for them.

Pixel's suspicions had been confirmed. Aranak had a motive for helping—and testing—them.

"We were chosen," Pixel deduced. He didn't know why he felt so certain. He just knew.

"Yes, you were chosen," Aranak smiled. "But I didn't choose you."

"Then why are you taking us in?" Pixel asked.

Aranak thought for a moment. "That's a question I can't directly answer at this moment. I promise you, before you leave my tower on the journey ahead of you, I will tell you. Right now, though, simply accept that I have a job to do. I am to train you in using your magic."

"Train?" asked Score. "As in lessons? School? That kind of stuff?"

"Essentially," agreed the wizard. He leaned forward. "You all have some ability to do magic. Changing tea into cola is one form of it, but all three of you possess the ability. It's my task to train you, so that you can call on your magic and use it."

"Perhaps you could explain this magic," Renald said slowly, echoing Pixel's thoughts. "Where I come from, magic is a trick, not something real."

"That is because you come from the Rim Worlds," Aranak answered. "I'm sure that on your worlds you have learned that planets revolve about stars and that there are vast distances between worlds?"

"Yeah," agreed Score. "On Earth, they've been sending rockets up to explore all these other planets. But none of them are like this place, I know that."

"That's where you are wrong," Aranak said firmly. "The way planets are arranged in space does not affect the Diadem."

"The what?" all three of them echoed together.

"The Diadem." The magician pressed his hands together, and smiled at them. "Imagine a layered sphere. The different layers—like those of an onion—are the different circuits of the Diadem. You can only travel from layer to layer by magic. You each come from three of the Rim Worlds, out on the edge. There are other Rim Worlds, too, around the edge of the sphere. True magic is very rare on the Rim Worlds. You three possess some, but there it was quite weak, and you could do only small things.

"Inside this outer layer of planets, the Rim Worlds, is another layer of worlds. This is the Outer Circuit. Treen—the world you are now on—is one of these worlds. Because it is closer to the heart of the Diadem, magic is stronger here. Your powers will be greater here than on your native worlds, but you now need to know how to focus and use them. That will be my task."

"So that's why I could turn an arrow into rose petals without touching it," Score observed. "We're closer to the source of true magic."

Pixel leaned forward. "And logically, then, there are other . . . circuits, as you called them, if this is the Outer Circuit. They must be closer to the center, and therefore possess even stronger magic."

"Correct." Aranak smiled approvingly. "Your understanding is very swift."

"Why do you stay here and not go to another world where your magic is more powerful?" Pixel wondered aloud.

For a moment, there was a look of annoyance on the magician's face, but he quickly wiped it off. "Because my own powers are limited. If I were to try to cross over to the Middle Circuit, it would drain me so thoroughly that I would be destroyed. I do not have enough magic to make it to the next level and still have sufficient power."

"Ah." Pixel nodded. Roughly translated, that meant that Aranak was probably the most powerful magician on this world—and if he went farther, he'd be a small fish in a big pond. He obviously liked being in command here.

"Now," said Aranak, "introductions, a brief lesson, and then I'm sure you'd all like to bathe and rest."

Renald nodded. "I am Renald. These are Pixel and Score. We already know your name."

"No," the magician replied, "you do not." At their looks of surprise, he smiled. "You know what I choose to have you call me."

"That's the same thing," Score objected.

"It is not." Aranak looked at them all very earnestly. "This is your first lesson in magic. To have power over something, you need three things: name, form, and substance. I am the Wizard of Names, because I know the true names of many things. To gain power over anything, a magician must first know its true name. In the case of an inanimate object, that is generally its common name." He gestured at the table. "For me to control that table, for example, I first need to know its true name is 'table.' To control people, you first need to know their true names. You will never be able to control me, no matter how strong you get, unless you discover my true name."

"Why would we want to control you?" asked Pixel. Again, it was just something he knew to ask.

"You won't," Aranak answered. "But my point is that you can't, unless you know my true name. So, your first lesson in magic is this: never give out your true names to a magic-user, as you did with me. I will not abuse that information, I promise you, but others might. In fact, they probably would. So be very careful in the future."

Pixel wasn't sure whether Aranak was telling the whole truth or not, but, for the moment, he was willing to accept what the magician said at face value. He was, after all, the resident expert in magic.

"Now, we'll continue lessons tomorrow," Aranak announced. "For the moment, I'm sure you'll want a wash, food, and rest. I've given each of you a room in the tower. Once you're trained, you'll be able to hop there by magic. For the moment, walking is probably the safest way. Follow me." He led them out of his study and into a long, bright corridor. "Most of the magic here works by itself. It's more convenient that way, naturally. But some things have to be triggered, and you won't be able to do that yet. For example, if you get into your baths, they'll automatically fill with water at just the right temperature. But you'll have to dry yourselves off with the towels I've provided."

He stopped beside a door. "Normally, my doors are invisible, but, for your convenience, I've made the ones you'll need solid for the time being. This is the dining room. You can order your food and drink in here. Anything my magic knows about will appear. I can't guarantee it's quite what you're used to on your home worlds, but if you experiment a bit you should be able to find something you like."

He led them to three more doors. "These are your rooms. Take whichever you prefer, for they are all alike. I'll see you in the morning for lessons. Good night." And he instantly vanished.

"That's going to take some getting used to," Score muttered. Then he shook himself. "I'll take this room," he decided. "Closest to the food." With a grin, he stepped inside.

Pixel and Renald looked at one another. "Take whichever you like," Pixel said generously. "They're all the same, after all."

"I'll take the farthest one," Renald announced. "If there is an attack, I shall be ready when they take you and Score."

"Cheerful thought," Pixel answered. "But I doubt anything can get in here."

"Don't be naive," Renald replied. "Aranak admitted there's a limit to his powers. Perhaps someone—or something—strange could get in here."

"Maybe," agreed Pixel. "But why would they want to?"

"Who knows?" Renald shrugged. "If magicians can do pretty much as they please, then they probably will do so."

With a sigh, Pixel walked into his room. Renald was a good fighter, but arrogant. Hopefully, the arrogance would not endanger them. And Score, too, was unpredictable. Not at all like Pixel's friends from home. He missed his old friends from the Net . . . even if he wasn't absolutely sure they were real.

Pixel's room was very simple, just the way he liked it. There was a bed, a chair, and a desk. In an alcove was the bath. They were all plain, just as they had been at home. Obviously magicians didn't need Virtual Reality. They could create their own realities if they wanted them.

Now that he thought about it, the idea of a nice, warm bath was very appealing. Pixel stripped off his dirty clothes and dropped them to the floor. He stepped into the empty bath, which was instantly full of warm, soapy water at just the perfect temperature. With a happy sigh, he settled back for a nice, long soak.

That lasted for about ten minutes. Just as he was really enjoying the soak—the water never got colder, or dirtier—he felt a sudden chill sweep over him. He bolted upright and stared in shock at the bathwater. It was bubbling and frothing, like a Jacuzzi, but without any reason. Worried, Pixel hopped out of the tub and wrapped a large, luxurious towel about himself.

The water was changing somehow. It seemed to be forming some kind of a waterspout, and was rising into the air in a solid, whirling mass. Pixel was too scared to look away. Something made it quite clear that this wasn't one of the room's little amenities. The column of water grew larger, and then took shape. It became human-looking, even down to having the features of a person. Pixel didn't want to look, but he couldn't drag his eyes away. The figure was a man, dressed in watery, flowing robes, and with a face that he somehow felt that he should know—

His father? There was definitely something of his father's face about the figure that seemed to be staring back at him with intense, watery eyes. Then, with a further shock, Pixel realized that he was wrong. It wasn't his father—it was him. This was an adult version of Pixel, a view of Pixel in the future.

Was this his fate? To be a real magician? With the power, perhaps, to send his younger self some warning or some message to help him?

"You're . . . you're me," he managed to gasp. "Aren't you?"

The figure didn't seem to be able to hear him. Instead, it gestured down at the surface of the tub in which it stood. Nervously, Pixel followed its indication.

In the water, he could see shapes and pictures . . . the portrait from his dream . . . other paintings. There was a sheet of paper, with writing on it, and then it vanished. In its place was a mass of bubbles, somehow all lined up and spelling a message:

/// > /+/+/

The bubbles burst, and the message was gone. Despite this, Pixel knew that it was somehow important. One hundred and eleven is greater than one plus one plus one. Well, obviously it was. Pixel didn't get it. Then he looked up to discover that the watery version of himself had vanished with the bubbles, and he was alone again.

If there had really been anything there to begin with. He toweled himself off and dressed again, thinking furiously. Had he just been sent a message from his future self? What did it mean?

Or was it some kind of trick, a trap from the beyond?

He didn't know, and he knew he'd never be able to figure it out alone. He needed help. And that meant talking to Renald and Score.

He walked to Renald's door. Pushing it open, he walked in.

Straight onto the point of Renald's sword. Pixel gulped as the point hovered at his throat, almost breaking the skin. Renald moved into view, half-dressed and furious.

"Never," Renald hissed, "do that again. You are not to enter my room. Is that clear?"

"Uh-huh," Pixel agreed. "I'd nod, but it might slit my throat. Can you put that away?"

After a moment, the sword moved. Renald sheathed it and stared at Pixel, still furious. "Now get out," the warrior ordered.

"I just had a weird thing happen to me," Pixel explained. "We need to talk about it."

Renald relented, saying, "I simply like my privacy, and will have it respected. I'll join you in the dining room when I'm dressed. Then we can talk."

Pixel ran into the dining room and found that Score had beaten him there. The other boy was frowning at a table half-filled with food. "Geez," he muttered. "They can't even produce a simple burger. Well, I'll have to do it the hard way." He picked up a piece of fowl, closed his eyes, and concentrated. He obviously was having fun with his own brand of magic. The drumstick in his hand shimmered for a second and then . . . became a live and flailing fish. With a cry of revulsion, Score threw it across the room.

Amused, Pixel couldn't resist commenting, "I think that was a little undercooked."

"Something went wrong," Score complained, fiercely wiping his hands on a napkin. "That wasn't what I was picturing at all."

"Then try again." Pixel picked up a piece of the bird and bit into it.

Score looked worried. "Nah . . . not until I know what went wrong. That's enough raw meat for me for one day." He looked up and ordered, "Another of what he's eating."

A second whatever-it-was leg appeared on the table, and Score started to eat it. Without complaining, for once.

"The weirdest thing just happened to me," Pixel announced, determined to try to find some explanation for what he had seen. "I just had something like a vision."

"Tell us." That was from Renald, who marched into the room.

Pixel replied, "It scared me, and it puzzled me. I wondered if either of you two could help me figure it out." He related what had happened and saw deep frustration on Renald's face.

"On our way here," Renald said slowly, "I, too, had a vision. I saw a page of paper, too, but couldn't read it. And I saw a book." Renald glanced at Pixel, puzzled. "It seems to be similar in one way to yours." Then they both looked at Score. "Have you, too, been seeing things?" Renald asked.

"Too many," Score answered. "But not like that." He reached into his pocket and pulled out a sheet of paper. "You want weird, look at this." He unfolded it and laid it on the table. "I found this in my place a couple of weeks ago." He tapped one line. "The same thing you saw in your bath," he pointed out.

"A hundred and eleven is greater than one plus one plus one," agreed Pixel. "It doesn't make any sense." His eyes narrowed as he saw the line. "Treen is the start," he breathed. "You knew about this place?"

"No," Score answered. "Just the name. When I first heard it, I almost died of shock." He stared hard at both of the others. "You know what this all means, don't you?"

"Yes," said Pixel, slowly. "It means that all of this was planned. It isn't just dumb luck that we're here. Somebody went to great lengths to get us to Treen. And that somebody is obviously using magical means to try and get messages to us."

Renald nodded. "These pages we've seen in visions must mean something." He gestured at the page that Score held. "That is only the first, clearly."

"And none of us understands this, do we?" Score pointed out.

"Some of it's obvious," Pixel replied. He gestured to a group of three characters. "Two males and a female, obviously, joined together. Maybe a group we're supposed to look out for?"

"Yes, but for what?" asked Score, frustrated. "Is it warning us against them or telling us to look for them?" He snorted. "Just about the only thing we can be sure of is that it doesn't refer to us. We're all male."

Pixel saw Renald's eyes narrow, as if he were considering something. But he didn't speak. Pixel couldn't make out what was wrong with the boy, but one thing was becoming clear. "We're all in this together," he said softly. “The three of us. We can’t work this out alone, so we have to work together. No matter how difficult it is. I think we’d better study hard with Aranak and learn as much as we can as fast as possible. Maybe then some of this will start to make sense.”

“Great,” muttered Score. “More school . . .”

Yes, Pixel thought, more school. Perhaps the only way to find out the truth was to give in fully to the magical realm.

7

Score couldn't help it—he was getting bored rapidly with their lessons. He supposed all this talk was necessary, but he wanted to get on and do something.

Aranak had begun telling them that to control magic, you had to focus your mind on it. "Fix in your mind whatever it is that you want to do or affect," he told them. "Know its name. Picture it clearly in your thoughts. Then reach out and touch it with your mind."

"What about spells?" demanded Pixel.

"You'll learn about those later," Aranak promised. "You can't run before you can walk. Or fly."

"I can already walk," grumbled Score. "You've seen me change things."

"Yes," agreed Aranak. "And Renald can foresee trouble. And Pixel can understand things. But none of you knows how those abilities work. You're acting instinctively, not consciously or thoughtfully. What you must do is *understand* what you can do before you can actually do it. So pay careful attention to me. Now, I want you all to practice visualizing with your mind." In front of each person, he set a glass and filled them magically with water. "Look at the glasses, and then close your eyes, picturing them as they are in your minds."

Reluctantly, Score did as he was told. This was so dull. He wanted to act. He closed his eyes, picturing the glass in his mind and trying to concentrate on it.

Suddenly, there was water all down his front.

With a yelp, he opened his eyes and saw that his glass had somehow tumbled over, and the water had drenched him. "Hey!" he complained. "How did that happen?" He knew the other two were laughing at him.

"You were not concentrating properly," Aranak informed him. "Your mind nudged the glass and spilled it. You must concentrate." He refilled the glass. "That's why we practice with small things first. Less can go wrong with them. Try again."

With a groan, Score focused harder on the picture in his mind. He was wet enough already.

"Now," he heard Aranak say, "open your eyes. Look at the glass, and then lift it, using just your mind."

Score opened his eyes, glared ferociously at the glass, and reached out to lift it, mentally.

It took off like a rocket, slammed into the ceiling, and shattered. He was soaked a second time, and there were pieces of blunted glass in with this drenching. He shook them out of his hair and off his clothing.

"Well," said Aranak, dryly, "at least you're enthusiastic." Renald and Pixel grinned at this, but the magician frowned at them. "I don't see either of you doing anything with your glasses."

That stopped them, and they turned back to stare nervously at their own glasses. Both wobbled uncertainly, splashing water on the table, but rose slowly into the air. Score could see the other two boys concentrating hard on keeping them there. They were looking so sure of themselves and superior, feeling that they'd put one over on him.

Angrily, Score reached out mentally again and tipped both glasses. Renald and Pixel yelled as they were suddenly soaked. Both looked confused until they saw his grin.

"You did that!" Renald accused, reaching for her sword.

"Leave that weapon alone!" stormed Aranak. "I think I had better forbid you to wear that in the Tower, young man. Yes, he did that. But if the two of you had been paying more attention to what you were doing, he wouldn't have been able to do it. Now, dry off, all of you." Three towels magically appeared. "Then we'll try again."

And so it went, for the rest of the morning. Small stuff, all of it, and it was so achingly slow that Score was bored out of his skull. After lunch, they returned to their studies. Score didn't feel that he was learning anything.

At the end of the afternoon, Aranak announced, "Well, the three of you are doing very well for your first day. I think that's enough for now. We'll resume tomorrow."

"When do we get to the good stuff?" demanded Score.

Aranak answered patiently, "You have to grasp the basics before you go further. Also, the more magic you use, the greater the likelihood of something going wrong."

"Wrong?" asked Pixel. "Like how?"

"If you try to tap into strong magic before you're ready to control it, then it might destroy you," the magician explained.

As Score, Renald, and Pixel walked back to the dining room for their afternoon meal, Score sighed. "Is it just me, or should we be doing something more interesting? Otherwise, what's the point of being able to do magic? And, don't forget, we decided we need to know as much as possible as fast as possible. I don't think Aranak shares that aim."

"No," agreed Pixel. "He's going very slowly and cautiously. We could be here forever at this rate. And I don't think we have forever."

Renald nodded. "I agree. It may be that Aranak is going slowly because he wants to build a solid base from which to work. Alternately . . ." Renald pondered. "It may be that he is simply attempting to gauge our powers, evaluating our potential. It is what a warrior would do with a potential foe."

"You think Aranak is our enemy?" asked Pixel.

"I do not know," Renald said simply. "But he is not truly our friend. I think we should be wary of him. And I agree with Score on one point. We should attempt to try our magic without Aranak's oversight. So, what did you have in mind?"

"I'm not sure yet," Score admitted. "But did you see all those books in Aranak's study? I'll bet there are some books of spells in there somewhere."

For a moment, he felt sure he saw Renald jerk slightly, as if what he had just said meant something to the other boy. But, whatever it was, he didn't mention it. "So you want to find a . . . book of spells and try it out?"

"Why not?" Score argued. "We'd probably have to get out of the Tower in order to do it. I'll bet Aranak would know if there's any other magic being conducted inside it."

Renald almost managed to crack a smile at that. "That's the first intelligent thing you've said. We need also to find a way out of the Tower. You may have noticed that the only doors we've seen are the ones to our rooms, the study, and the dining hall."

They had reached the latter by now and ordered up food for themselves.

Pixel nodded. "So there's probably some magical way out of the Tower," he pointed out. "We need to find out what it is. But," he added cautiously, "we may not be safe out there. Those villagers might still be hanging around."

"This close to Aranak's Tower?" sneered Score. "They wouldn't dare. Anyway, I don't think we need to go too far. Maybe just a half mile or so." He changed his tea to cola. "Besides, we need to know if we're here of our own free will or if we are prisoners."

"Also," Renald pointed out, "Aranak did say that we shouldn't try to handle too much magic at once. It might turn on us, as it did to Hakar. I think we should try to do something small to start with, in case it doesn't work right."

Score noticed that the other boys seemed to have agreed to be a part of his plan. He grinned. "I'll bet Aranak is worried that we'll get too good too fast. I mean, I caught him by surprise when I tipped your drinks over earlier."

"Which reminds me that I owe you for that," Renald replied. "And I shall pay you back . . . later."

Score wasn't too worried about that threat. He was certain that, of the three of them, he was the strongest magic-user. He could do the changing magic, for example, which they couldn't yet. And he had taken control of their glasses from them. Renald might be good with his sword, but Score probably had the advantage when it came to magic. "Well," he admitted, "you may be right about trying something small tomorrow. Just as long as it could be fun, too."

"No problem with that," Pixel agreed. "So—do we check out the library after dinner?"

"Sounds good to me," Score said. "There's no TV here, and nothing much else to do in the evening. Unless you guys want to shoot some hoops."

Renald frowned. "You do not have any weapons. What will you shoot these 'hoops' with? And what is 'TV'?"

Score sighed. Renald was such a drag. "Forget it," he muttered. "How about the library instead?"

"I'm all for it," agreed Pixel. "We shouldn't waste any time."

They finished their food, and then walked back to the library. There they stopped, puzzled.

There was no longer a door.

After a minute, Pixel said, "I guess that means keep out. We may as well go back."

"Do you always give up so easily?" asked Renald scornfully. "We know that there is a door here because we have used it."

"But it's not here now," Pixel objected. "So we can't go in."

"No," said Renald firmly. "The door *must* be here now. It just isn't visible. All we have to do is make it appear."

Score grinned. For once, he realized, Renald had come up with a good idea. "Right. All we need to do is concentrate on making the door appear. That should be enough."

"Agreed," Renald said. "Now—all together."

Score was briefly irritated that Renald had taken command again. But there wasn't any point in objecting right this moment. The important thing was to get the door open. So he concentrated, picturing the door that he knew was there to be visible.

After a few seconds, the door was suddenly there again.

"All right!" he crowed happily, opening it. "We did it. We must be pretty slick magic-users, after all."

Renald gave him a "what a joke" look. "Overconfidence can get you killed."

"So can an attitude problem," Score snapped back. "Let's take a look at those books." He didn't wait to see what Renald would do, but hurried over to the nearest bookcase. He started reading the titles on the spines of the books, but none of them seemed to be at all on magic. *Changaron*, said one. What was that? He opened it, to discover it was some kind of story, printed in a language he'd never seen before. The next book was *The Tale of Tomai.* "Great," he muttered to himself. "This must be the adventure story section." The next book had a title that made no sense at all: *Cigam fo Koob Eht.* Probably in some weird foreign language.

He glanced at his companions, to see if they were having any more luck. Renald was standing in the middle of the room, a vacant expression on his face. Score's first thought was that the kid was goofing off; but then he realized that Renald would never do something so frivolous. He frowned. Maybe he was having another of his visions again?

Then Renald snapped back to attention. "It just happened again," he said, confirming Score's guess. "I saw the book again. It must be close. And I saw a page like Score has being placed in it."

"Can you see it here anywhere?" Score asked him, excitedly. Maybe they were onto something at last!

"No," Renald said with a sigh. "It isn't here."

"Then we'd better continue," Score said, deflated.

After about five more minutes, Pixel called out, excitedly, "I think this is something." The others hurried over to see what Pixel had found.

It was a normal-looking shelf of books, but the books had rearranged themselves into a pattern:

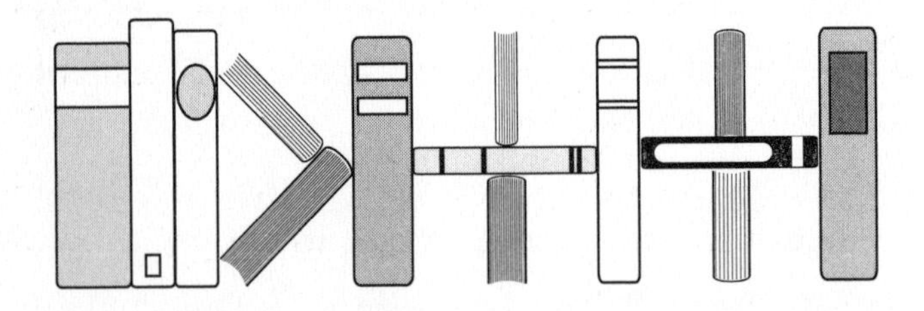

"Bingo," breathed Score. Pixel took down the first book on the shelf and opened it.

It was unlabeled and written in a weird-looking script. It was quite slim, only about forty pages long. But the page Pixel had it open to was labeled, "Calling." Score skimmed it over Pixel's shoulder and saw from the illustrations that it was instructions on how to conjure an animal forward. Unfortunately, it was written in code.

"I'm sure this is the right sort of thing," Pixel said excitedly. "There are other pages about transmuting liquids, seeing into the future, and stuff."

"Yeah," Score said, not wanting to get his hopes up too high, "but maybe it's fiction."

"There is only one way to know, and that is if we try one of the spells." Renald examined the shelf, pulling out a second slender volume. "This appears to be similar."

Score looked over the books, too, and found a third small, green tome. "And here's another. There's probably lots more."

"Yes, but these three should be sufficient," Renald argued. "We can each read one tonight, and then tomorrow we can agree on which spell to try."

"Sounds good to me," agreed Pixel, happy to have been the one to make their find. "Maybe we should go now, before Aranak finds us in here."

"Agreed." Once more, Renald had taken the lead. Score felt another flash of annoyance—he felt shoved aside.

Outside, Renald indicated for the others to halt. "We had better lose this door again, or else Aranak will know for certain we have been in here."

"He probably knows anyway," Score objected. "He's a magician, after all."

"We may assume that he does," agreed Renald. "But there is no reason to make our actions absolutely clear, is there? Now, concentrate on getting rid of the door."

Again, it wasn't worth a fight. Score sighed, and focused on the wall being absolutely smooth again.

And the door vanished, as if there never had been one.

"Well," Score said, "I've had about as much of you two as I can take for one day. I'm going to my room to study now." Ignoring their looks, he hurried off. He could hardly wait to discover some real magic at last!

8

Renald was considerably irritated at the start of the following day. She had spent the evening studying the book she had found, growing more and more annoyed. There were spells in it, to be sure, but not ones that were of any use to a warrior. She had no desire to know how to remove warts or cast a love spell or get rid of mice. These were the sort of things that the good wives of her world were supposed to be able to do, and they had always seemed totally pointless to her. Also, some of the spells—probably the most important ones—were written in an incomprehensible code.

What she wanted was some idea of how to control the powers Aranak insisted she possessed—and to be able to use them for fighting. She didn't quite know why, but she was certain that there was trouble ahead. Those attackers in her father's castle had been only the first move in some great game of war. There would soon come a second, and she wanted to be ready. And this book of minor spells was of absolutely no use to her.

Well, perhaps Score or Pixel had better luck with their books. They needed something to give them an advantage here. Renald didn't like the idea of depending on either boy for anything. Still, for some reason, she knew her fate was linked with theirs.

Briefly, she recalled that strange person, Cleora, who had warned her that she would need help. Was he behind all of this? There was no way to know yet, so she turned her attention to other matters as she prepared for her morning lessons with Aranak.

At least Pixel had taken her seriously about not entering her room unannounced. She had barely managed to keep her secret from him the first time, and it was important that he not have any other opportunity to discover that she was really female. Actually, Renald wasn't completely sure why that should be. After all, as far as she knew, on his world girls were allowed to become warriors as much as boys. Still, she didn't feel like taking that chance, and she had absolutely no reason to trust Pixel to keep quiet if he discovered the truth.

And even less if Score did.

Renald was disappointed they hadn't found the book from her dreams. She was sure it was nearby. But where? It had to be something very valuable, so Aranak—if he knew what it was worth—would have it hidden away somewhere. She couldn't explain her own feeling of certainty, but there was definitely something here . . .

With a sigh, she gave up all of the useless thoughts and went along to her lesson with Pixel and Score. As on the previous day, Aranak awaited them in his study. If he knew about the missing books, he gave no indication. The three of them hadn't mentioned the books this morning, in case he might overhear them, but from the glum expressions on their faces, Renald could tell the boys had had no more luck than she.

The morning's lessons were as slow as ever. More basic skills, but nothing with any immediate prospect of being useful. Renald also noticed that they were being taught nothing that would be helpful in a fight. The most exciting thing that happened was when Aranak had them use their power to hatch chicks out of eggs. Score, naturally, tried to outdo the others and produced a large, angry rooster. Renald still had her sword, despite Aranak's threat, and used it to lop off the bird's head.

"Dinner," she announced. That prompted Aranak to dismiss them for food.

As they headed off to the dining room, Renald had to admit that she felt drained. Doing magic wasn't really like doing work, since it was all done through the powers of the mind tapping into the force that magic provided. But it definitely drained her strength. They had yet to reach the upper limits of their power, which was an intriguing sign. She had the distinct impression that Aranak was secretly very impressed with their potential.

As they ate, she asked the others about the magic books. She told them how useless her own was.

"Mine too," agreed Score, through a mouthful of one of his transmuted hamburgers and fries. "All stupid stuff about finding lost items of jewelry and repairing broken fingernails. Stuff girls would want to know—not us."

Renald's hackles rose at the contemptuous way he said "girls." Then she caught herself and tried to shrug it off. "What about you?" she asked Pixel.

The thin boy blinked and snapped back to attention. He'd been watching her closely for some reason. "Me? Well, the spells are a lot like the ones you found. On the other hand, I've been thinking about the first one. You know, the one that will call an animal to you."

"An animal?" Score scoffed. "Big deal."

"Agreed," Pixel admitted. "But it's a good test, wouldn't you say? If we try the spell to bring, say, a dog to us, and a dog appears, we'll know we can do it. This is, after all, just a trial. However, there is a problem with the spell."

"And that is?" asked Renald, irritated. Why hadn't he mentioned this at the start?

Pixel looked uncomfortable. "I don't understand it," he admitted. He opened the book and showed it to them. "I was hoping that we might make sense of it together."

Renald and Score looked down at the spell. Renald blinked, and stared. It read:

HZB GSV MZNV LU GSV XIVGFIV
RM GSRH NZMMVI GL XZ00

"Some kind of foreign or magical language?" suggested Score. "Huzub gesev . . ." his voice trailed off. "We're never going to be able to read that, let alone try to remember it."

"It looks more like some kind of code to me," Renald offered. "We use various codes to send messages that we don't want other people to be able to make out."

"Right," agreed Pixel. "That's what I thought. It's probably some sort of substitution system, where one letter stands for a different letter. Then all you need to know is which ones. That's where the problem comes in. If it's random, then we'll have real trouble trying to figure it out. I mean, the obvious thing is that the letters are either replaced by the one before it or the one after it in the alphabet. But that doesn't work here."

Score frowned as he concentrated. "The most common letter in English is *E*," he said. "The most common letters in that line are G and *V*. So one of them should be *E*."

"G starts a couple of three-letter words," Renald added. "So I don't think that could be it. *V* is most likely."

Pixel snapped his fingers. "There are two words repeated in this short sentence," he said excitedly. "'*GSV.*' And if *V* is *E*, we have a common three-letter word ending in *E*. 'The'!"

Renald nodded. "But it doesn't help much," she pointed out. "G is *T*; *S* is *H*; and *V* is *E*. There doesn't seem to be any kind of pattern there."

"Wait a minute," Score said. "There is something. G is *T*. Then the second letter is *S*, which is *H*. *S* and *T*, G and *H*. Both are together in the alphabet."

"That's it!" Pixel said happily. "That's the clue, Score. It's a reversed alphabet." Seeing the blank stares of the others, he explained. "Take a sheet of paper, and write the alphabet down, *A* to *Z*. Then, underneath it, write the alphabet down from *Z* to *A*. So *A* becomes *Z*, G becomes *T*, and *Z* becomes *A*."

"You've solved it," Score replied, looking happier.

"*We* solved it together," Pixel answered. "We worked the thing out together." He was scribbling furiously on a loose sheet of paper. "Right, I've done that, so let's decode the message and see what it says." He went to work and a couple of minutes later grinned up at them. "It says, 'Say the name of the creature in this manner to call.' So we just have to translate 'dog.'

That becomes . . . *WLT*. So if we say that, we should be able to call up a dog."

"Terrific." Score nodded. "Now, how do we get out of the Tower?"

"The same way we got into the Tower," Renald suggested. "We find a place where a door should be and use the code. Come on."

They quickly walked the corridors until they found themselves at a place where the glasslike wall was thinner. Renald could just make out shapes of trees through the dusky glass. "Here," she said firmly. She pressed her hand against the wall.

A message appeared.

TYPE COMMAND

"Allow me," Pixel said, using his finger to trace his response onto the wall:

This time, the castle responded.

ARE YOU SURE

Pixel studied the words for a moment, then wrote a response:

YES

Suddenly, they were all standing outside, bathed in the red glow of sunset.

Pixel gestured toward the start of the woods about a hundred yards away. "How about there? We'll be out of sight, at least."

"Out of nonmagical sight," pointed out Renald. "Aranak could be watching us right now, you know."

Pixel shrugged. "If he is, he is. There's not much we can do about it, is there?" He started off toward the woods, Score keeping pace with him. Renald hung back slightly, staring hard at the Tower.

Out of the corner of her eye, Renald saw a flicker. She turned just as the flicker was fading. The afterglow was the shape of a man. She was reminded of the strange figure who had betrayed her on Ordin.

Or maybe Aranak was watching them. It would be a smart move, especially if he didn't trust the trio. But how smart was the magician? Renald didn't know. True, he knew a lot about magic, but knowledge and wisdom were two different things. Then, realizing Pixel and Score were almost out of sight, she started after them.

When the three of them were far enough from the Tower, they halted. Pixel opened the book to the spell. "Well, maybe we should get on with this, while there's still enough light to read by."

The other two gathered behind him, reading over his shoulder. "I think we have to just picture a dog," Pixel explained, "and then say *WLT* together, reaching out with our minds to make the calling."

"Geez," groused Score. "You sound just like Aranak. Let's just get on with it, okay?"

Together, the three of them concentrated and, on Pixel's signal, they all said "*WLT*," loudly and firmly. Renald kept her mind focused on the image of a dog, one of the wolfhounds that her father kept for hunting.

Then the spell was done, and Renald felt something like a puff of energy go out of her. "I think it's working," she said. "I felt something."

"Me, too," agreed Pixel, closing the book and slipping it back into his trouser pocket. "I wonder how long we have to wait."

No sooner had he asked this than he was answered. From the growing gloom came the howl of a wolf.

"Uh-oh," muttered Score nervously. "I've got a bad feeling about this."

"Me, too," agreed Pixel, looking just as scared. "That was a wolf, right?"

"Yes," agreed Renald, drawing her sword and peering through the twilight. "But they travel in packs."

As if to underscore her point, there were answering howls from around them.

"I think we'd better go back to the Tower," Score said nervously.

"Great idea," Renald replied scornfully. "Except that's the direction the howls are coming from. They've cut off our retreat." She didn't take her eyes off the opening in the trees for a second. "And I think they're getting closer."

Score was sweating, he was so scared. "Now what?" he asked, his voice squeaky with fear.

"I think we had better fall back," Renald suggested softly. "Both of you, head back into the woods. Look for areas of dense brush, because wolves won't enter that. Or a cave or something we can defend. And look out for fallen branches that you can use as clubs. I'll watch our backs. Now move!"

Slowly, the three of them retreated. Renald kept scanning the trees as they passed deeper into the woods. There were ominous rustlings, and she was certain that she'd caught a glimpse of several long, lean shapes.

"What went wrong?" Pixel muttered. "Did we mess up and call wolves? Or did the magic just go wrong?"

Renald remembered she'd been thinking of wolfhounds . . . Had she accidentally summoned the wolves? She didn't want to think about the possibility. Maybe the magic was corrupt.

The wolves' attack came swiftly. One huge wolf, dark furred, with a gray streak down his back, leaped snarling from the bushes straight for Pixel.

9

Pixel almost fainted as the ravenous creature hurled itself at him. He'd picked up a stick, but after that he was paralyzed with shock and fear. All he could see were the huge, slavering fangs of the wolf as it came at him.

There was a flash of action as Renald's sword slammed into the side of the monster. There was a spray of blood and the stench of it in the air. Renald pulled the sword out of the falling, dead animal and was on the alert again in seconds.

"Let's go," Renald yelled to Pixel. "We've got to fight for our lives!"

Pixel managed to wrench himself into action as the wolf's corpse landed at his feet. Terror impelled him into motion. Heart pounding, sick to his stomach, he raised his makeshift club. Beside him, Score did the same. Keeping up their retreat, they looked around them. Thankfully, there had been a short pause after the lone attack. But then the furious growling resumed, and dark, lean shapes flew forward.

Pixel had to force himself to fight, whipping the stick around and clubbing at the closest wolf with it. The animal yelped as he smacked it smartly across the snout, probably more from surprise and irritation than actual pain. But at least it now hesitated before attacking.

This was far too much like the dog attack he'd barely escaped from. That had been the only other time in his life when he'd faced physical danger. In his VR travels, of course, he'd overcome danger many, many times. But that had been different, because he had always known he couldn't be really hurt in the computer-generated world. Here he could not only be hurt, he could be killed.

He struck out again at another wolf. As he did so, a third whipped forward from his right, grabbing at his stick with its powerful jaws. Pixel was shocked, realizing that these wolves were very smart. They knew that without his weapon he would be helpless. And he couldn't pull it free from the snarling, hungry wolf. He saw the second wolf getting ready to spring toward him, and he was defenseless.

Unless . . . Pixel's mind was working ahead of him again. Instinctively, he thought of fire. He had to conjure fire.

"*Shriker Kula prior*," he chanted. The words just appeared—he didn't have to think of them. Suddenly, there was fire.

The end of his stick burst into a blaze of leaping flame. Pixel whirled the blazing stick around in a circle, and the wolves backed off, fear in their eyes.

"All right!" Pixel grinned in triumph. He chanced a quick glance around, now that he could see properly in the flickering firelight. Renald had killed another wolf, and two more were circling warily just outside of the range of his sword. On the other side, Score was shaking with fear as he swatted at two more wolves, who were lunging for his stick.

Pixel yelled, "Make fire!" and waved his own stick to emphasize his point. Startled, Score got the message. He recited Pixel's chant, and a second later, the end of his own stick burst into flames. The two wolves, snarling, retreated from the fire.

That made Score grin. "Let's do better than that," he muttered, concentrating again.

A bush to one side of them erupted in a sheet of fire that made the wolves howl and scurry away. Pixel yelped, too, as he jumped back to avoid being singed. Renald slid back to join them as Score ignited another bush to the other side of their path.

The wolves stayed beyond the flames, their eyes glowing in the light. With several of the wolves already dead, they evidently decided to look for something easier to hunt. One by one, they melted away into the night.

"Not bad," Renald admitted, giving Pixel an appraising glance. "A good tactical move. How did you know the words?"

"They just came to me," Pixel shrugged modestly. "Hey, we have this magic, so I figured we should use it."

"Overuse it," Renald corrected. "The fire's spreading."

It was indeed. Several more bushes and one of the nearby trees were now on fire, and the heat was forcing them to retreat farther and farther from the Tower. More trees ignited in the flames, and Pixel realized that there was quite a blaze going now.

"It's a pity we don't know any firefighting spells," he muttered.

"This way," Renald decided, gesturing toward a path. "We'd better get out of here really fast." For once, even Score didn't argue, and the three of them hurried down the path.

Pixel was still shaking from his close encounter with death. He realized just how unprepared he was to live in any sort of a real world. And this one was getting a little bit too real for his liking. He preferred his danger and excitement the virtual way. At least that didn't kill you. On the other hand, he realized that Renald was obviously having fun. For once, the usually grim-faced youth had the flicker of a smile on his face.

There was something about Renald that was tugging at the edges of Pixel's mind, but he couldn't quite put his finger on it.

"Is this far enough yet?" Pixel called ahead, winded. He wasn't used to so much activity.

Renald glanced backward. There was now just the suggestion of dancing flames far off in the woods. "Yes," Renald said, reluctantly. "I suppose we'd better go on at a slower pace."

Score looked relieved, too, as they slowed to a walk. Then he asked, "Are you sure that this is the way back to the Tower?"

"No," admitted Renald, glancing up at the stars. "But it is away from the fire. I don't recognize any of the constellations, so there's no way I can navigate. We'll just have to wait until sunrise, and take our bearings then."

"If the sun rises in the east on this planet," Score grumbled.

Renald looked startled, and replied grimly, "It rises in the west on mine."

"And the north on mine," Pixel put in helpfully.

"So who knows where it will rise here?" He sighed, feeling even more depressed. "So we're completely lost, then?"

"We'll manage," Renald said, refusing to give up hope. "Maybe we'll run into one of the Bestials. They must live somewhere in these woods."

Pixel shrugged. It was worth hoping for, he supposed.

The next second, something large and heavy pushed him to the ground, dazing him. As his head started to clear, he realized that he couldn't get up. There was some sort of netting over him. He tried to stand, looking around in alarm as he did so.

The three of them were under the one net, which had been dropped over them from the trees. Men leaped from the bushes, tightening the grip of the net. Several of them managed to subdue and disarm Renald. In the crowd of men, Pixel recognized the leader of the party who had attacked them a few days before, when they had first arrived on this world.

"So," the man growled, "our information was correct, then. You young magic-users are finally in our hands. And, just to make certain you don't pull any stupid tricks . . ." He signaled the men. Pixel looked around, alarmed, but then something heavy and painful slammed into the back of his head, and he lost consciousness.

When Pixel awoke, his head felt like it was splitting. He rose groggily with one unsteady elbow. After his head stopped aching and the bright flashes of yellow pain had died down, he opened his eyes and groaned.

"About time you woke up," Renald was irritated at their capture. "Come on, get together."

"My head hurts," he complained, trying to sit up. He looked around. He, Renald, and the sullen-looking Score were all inside a very small room. The walls were made of stone, and there was just a small window, high up on one wall, much too small to get out of. There was a large door, with a lock, and straw on the stone floor. Pulling bits of straw from his hair, he finally managed to sit up. At least he didn't have to ask where they were. The answer to that was pretty obvious. "The villagers captured us."

"Somebody betrayed us to them," Renald replied. "And I've got a good idea who it must have been. I think I might have seen this man named Cleora, who betrayed me back on my own world, and it looks like he's doing the same here. Perhaps he's Aranak's tool."

That's weird," Score spoke up. "A stranger got me into trouble on Earth."

"And me on mine," added Pixel. He rubbed his sore head. "It looks like some people want us dead very badly, for some reason."

"Then some people will be very happy soon," said a gloating voice from the door. Pixel looked around and saw that a small hatch had opened in the door, just large enough for a face to peer in. Pixel wasn't too surprised to see the face of the village leader. "In the morning, we're going to take you to the fires."

Pixel swallowed. It was every bit as bad as he'd been fearing. "Why?" he asked. His voice sounded like a whine, and he winced.

"Best to kill you before you get too strong to be killed," replied the man. "Filthy magic-users."

Score grimaced. "Yeah, well, we don't exactly love you, either. Can we at least get some water? I'm dying of thirst."

The man laughed. "I promise you, thirst is one thing you won't die from." He slammed the hatch shut. Pixel heard his laughter fading as he went away.

"Terrific." Renald sat down on the floor. "Now what do we do?"

"We get out of here," Pixel replied. "If we don't, we're going to get turned into well-done steaks."

"It's easy to say get out of here," Renald snapped. "But how do you propose we do it?"

Score obviously resented Renald's tone. "Look, just because you were born the son of a noble on your world doesn't make you any better than us, you know!"

Renald snorted in contempt. "I'm better than you in every possible way. Would you like to fight?"

Pixel sighed. "Can't you think of anything other than violence?" he asked. "It doesn't matter how strong you are, or how good you are with a sword, or how many men you've killed. None of that will get us out of this room. So both of you—stop it. You're not helping."

Pixel thought Renald would put up a fight, maybe even attack him. But to his surprise, Renald held up his hands. "Enough," the warrior said calmly. "I could beat you senseless, but what's the point? You've got more courage than I gave you credit for, that's for certain. I apologize."

"You what?" Score asked, not believing his ears.

"I apologize," Renald repeated. "Fighting amongst ourselves isn't going to solve anything."

Pixel turned his glance to Score.

"Well," Score said slowly, "I guess you're right."

"Okay, then," Pixel said, glad the tense moment had passed. "We're still in this cell, remember, and in my appointment book is a date with a fire in the morning. How do we get out of here?" He walked slowly to the door and examined it. This had to be their way out. They could never get through the stone walls or the tiny window.

The villager had mentioned men on guard, but maybe they could be dealt with separately. What they needed first was to be on the other side of this door. The villagers had carefully taken anything that might be used as a weapon, even down to allowing them no water or food. And without something to work on, it didn't much matter that they could do magic. Even Renald's weapons had been taken away. All they had were the clothes they stood up in.

Score tried to change the lock, the way he had changed the cards in his Earth life. But the magic wouldn't work. He could change the kind of metal of the lock, but he couldn't weaken it.

And then an idea came to Pixel. He bent to examine the lock. "Lead, most likely," he muttered. "Cheap and easy to make." With a sudden grin, he turned back to the others, who had stood watching him in silence. "Fire," he announced. "Something we can all do."

"It won't work," Renald protested. "If we try to burn down the door, the straw will ignite, and we'll probably go up in flames with it. I'd rather not do the villagers' work for them."

"We don't burn the door down," Pixel said patiently. "We set the fire in the lock. It's lead, and lead melts at 327 degrees. We should be able to get the straw to burn that hot without any problem if we combine our powers." He started gathering up straw and stuffing it into the lock. "With the lock melted, we can get out of this room. Then we find the way out and take on the guards." He gave Renald a smile. "That'll be your part, of course. Two armed men should be really easy for you to take out, right?"

That actually brought a grin to the fighter's face. "It will not be a problem."

Score scowled at the door. "If we melt the lock, do you think it might set fire to some of the straw?"

"I don't think so," Pixel answered. "But we can do something about it. All we need to do is put something on the floor under the lock to catch any drips."

He glanced at Renald. "How about your cap?"

"No!" Renald exclaimed, looking more worried than annoyed.

"Why not?" Score asked.

Slowly, Pixel began to realize . . . the look on Renald's face when Score had made fun of "girl things"

. . . the way Renald's voice sometimes lifted . . . Renald's privacy . . . the reason Renald wouldn't take off the cap . . .

"You're a girl aren't you?" Pixel asked.

Renald went red and then narrowed his eyes. "What makes you think that?"

"It's obvious," Pixel replied. "I figured it out."

"A girl?" Score said, clearly astonished. "Renald is a girl? I've been pushed around by a girl?"

"Yes," growled Renald, taking off her cap. Her long, brown hair cascaded down about her shoulders. "And I can still beat you up, don't forget."

"A girl," Score repeated again.

"Oh, shut up," Pixel told him. "So she's a girl. Big deal. She's still the best fighter among us, and if you can't cope with that, tough." He took the cap that Renald offered him and slid it into place under the lock. "Now, if we can all get back into gear, let's get to work. Unless you want to be burned at the stake."

Score stared at Renald again, and then shook his head. "But I'm not taking any more orders from her," he insisted. "No girl bosses me around."

"How about we leave you here instead then?" suggested Renald, with mock sweetness.

"Give me a break," muttered Pixel. What was wrong with the Earth boy? It really didn't make any difference whether Renald was a boy or a girl. "Get it together now, okay? All together, concentrate."

He focused his mind and recited the chant. Beside him, Renald and Score did the same.

In a huge blaze of fire, the straw ignited. There was a brief fury of flame, and then bits of molten lead dripped onto the door. Renald, a grin on her face, kicked out at the door. It whipped open and she dived through it, ready for trouble. Pixel couldn't help admiring her a little as he followed.

They were in a short stone corridor. This had to be the local jail, he supposed. At the end of this corridor was another door. Locked or unlocked? Renald tried it, and it opened. She dashed through into the next room.

There were two armed men in the room, relaxing over some kind of drinks in large mugs. They leaped to their feet, their hands going to the swords they wore stuck through their belts. Then they realized that one of the escaped prisoners was— "A girl!" one of them exclaimed, his sword barely raised. He frowned, and Renald took advantage of his hesitation. Her hand went out, closing around the wrist that held his sword.

Spinning about, she applied leverage and spun him across her shoulder and down to the floor. She gave his wrist a twist as he squealed and flew through the air. Pixel heard his wrist bones snap, and now Renald had a weapon.

The other man wasn't going to give her the chance to use it. Her back was toward him, and he lunged at her with his own sword.

Pixel didn't have time to think if he didn't want Renald to be killed. He reached out with his mind and set the man's trousers on fire.

The man screamed, his lunge for Renald going very wide as he batted at his blazing pants. Pixel snatched up one of the mugs the men had been drinking from and threw the contents over the man's painful blaze. As he did so, Renald used the edge of her stolen sword to knock him out.

"Nasty," she commented, with a grin. "You're really learning, aren't you?" She sounded almost approving for once.

Score pushed past them. "Let's get out of here before anyone else comes," he said.

"Not yet," Renald answered firmly. She went to the cupboard in the corner and opened it. She smiled in delight when she saw that her swordbelt and knife were there. She tossed the borrowed sword aside. "I'm not going anywhere without my good weapons. That one was a piece of garbage. It'd break in a real fight."

"Please hurry," demanded Score. "The sooner we're out of here, the cooler I'll feel. I can almost feel those flames from here."

Renald finished arming herself, slipping the knife into the top of her boot. "Ready," she said. Pixel considered picking up her discarded sword, but decided against it. He didn't know how to use one, and he'd be better off without a weapon he wasn't used to. Besides, he was doing okay with his magic!

They slipped out of the jail and into the darkness. It had to be past midnight, and the village was virtually deserted. The villagers were going to be in for a surprise when they checked out the jail in the morning. Under cover of darkness, Renald, Pixel, and Score hurried out of the village and back into the woods again. They didn't speak a word for almost twenty minutes, when Pixel was forced to call for a halt again, a painful stitch in his side.

"Sorry," he gasped. "I've got to rest."

Together, Renald, Pixel, and Score stepped off the path they'd been walking on into a grove of trees. Renald said there was something familiar about the place, like her world—and then she saw the strange purple tree.

"Anyway, it'll be safer to wait here," she suggested brusquely. "That way, we'll see if anyone approaches us."

That's wise advice you give, my dear
I'm glad to see that you're all here.

Pixel whirled around, and saw, "Relcoa!"

At the same instant, Renald yelped, "Cleora!"

And Score finished off with, "LeCora!"

10

Score stood paralyzed as the black-clad, flickering man bowed and smiled.

I am all three—one in the same
Yet none of you has my true name.

Score frowned and studied the man who had gotten him into all this trouble. It was obvious that he had to be here to create more problems for them. "Why don't we all jump him?" he suggested. "He's the one who ratted on me."

"And on me," added Renald.

"And almost fed me to the dogs," Pixel finished. "I don't think we should trust him.

Score shook his head. "You must be crazy if you think any of us would trust you," he said. But he held back on actually attacking the man.

You must begin to trust in me.
I know much more than you can see.

The man stared earnestly at them. "Give us a reason to trust you," challenged Pixel. "Tell us something that might actually help us for once."

The man nodded.

Death awaits not far from here.
Each of you has much to fear.
Travel down this path with care,
You will find the Tower there.
But do not rest at journey's end,
For Aranak is not your friend.

"Aranak?" Score repeated, shaking his head in disbelief. "He's been teaching us magic and showing us how to control it. Why would he do that if he's our enemy?"

His motives only he can know
And he is not your greatest foe.

What he will say will be a lie.
Trust me or you will surely die.

Renald shook her head. "But you're the one who always seems to bring us trouble," she objected. The man shrugged.

Again I say, you're in my care.
Your worries and your dreams I share.
The changelings don't deserve your trust.
Though kindly, they do what they must.
They follow orders and have said
Their masters want to see you dead.

"Marvelous," muttered Pixel. "So you're telling us that we can trust nobody but you?" He gave a sharp laugh. "Forgive me, but I find that hard to accept."

Believe but in yourselves, my friends.
Your destiny on this depends.
Now, to the Tower everyone.
Night's ending with tomorrow's sun.

Score laughed incredulously. "You try and tell us that Aranak is our enemy, and then tell us to go back to him? Aren't you contradicting yourself just a little here?"

Relcoa/Cleora/LeCora shook his head, a slight smile still on his lips. He looked straight at Renald.

Go to him, but hide away,
He plans to kill you all today.
His Tower holds a thing most rare,
The Book of Names is hidden there.
It's opposite reveals to you.
A magic that will see you through.

Renald gave a start. "The Book of Names?" she repeated, staring at him. Score gave her a look. "It's the one I've been dreaming about, the one that contains a page," she explained. "I feel certain it is in the Tower. But how does Cleora know about my dreams?"

"Beats me," Score said. He thought for a moment. "The book must be hidden in the library." He glanced at the stranger sharply. "That doesn't mean I believe everything you say," he warned the man. "Just this one bit of it."

Pixel nodded. "It does make sense," he agreed. "And if we can find that, then maybe we can learn some stuff that will actually help us."

When one is finally made of three
Cosmic power will be set free.

The man gestured again in the direction that he claimed the Tower lay. Score glanced around, and when he looked back, the man was gone.

"I hate it when he does that," Score muttered. He glanced at his companions. "So, what do we do now? Do you believe that guy?"

"No," said Renald firmly. "I fear we'd be making a big mistake if we did. But he wants us back at the Tower, and we want to be back at the Tower. So . . ." She started off in the indicated direction, then smiled at Score. "Of course, if you have problems following a girl, you're welcome to take some other road."

Score flushed, irritated again. It had been bad enough for him when he'd thought she was a boy. A male Renald had been a big enough pain. Now, to discover she was a girl, as well! It only made her harder to take. On the other hand, she appeared to be leading in the right direction. Sullenly, he fell into step with Pixel.

After about fifteen minutes, Pixel suddenly said, "I wonder why Relcoa uses so many different names."

"Because he's trying to con us," Score suggested. "He's a liar, through and through."

"I'm not so sure," Pixel argued. "If he wanted to con us, why did he appear to all of us at once, instead of waiting till we're separated?"

Score snorted. "Because we're hardly ever separated."

"We are nearing the Tower," Renald said. "Thank goodness."

"Right," agreed Pixel. "I think he deliberately used different names for some reason." Then he snapped his fingers. "Of course! Our first lesson in magic—when you know something's true name, then you have power over it. We know his names, but we don't know his true name."

It made a kind of weird sense to Score, and that worried him. Was he actually starting to get used to this magic stuff? "But he used three names," he complained. "LeCora, Cleora, and Relcoa. Which of them is the true one?"

"Probably none of them," Renald suggested. "I think they're all fakes."

"Marvelous," Score complained. "Then we're no better off than we were. His name could be anything."

"Yes," agreed Pixel, excitedly. "But I don't think it is. I think all the fake names are pointing us to his real name." Seeing Score's blank expression, he explained. "Haven't you noticed that all the three aliases he gave us contain exactly the same letters? *L—E—C—O—R—A*. That means he's either very unimaginative or else he's giving us a clue as to his real name."

"If he wanted us to know it," Score objected, "why didn't he just tell us?"

Pixel shrugged. "Maybe for the same reason he always speaks in rhymes. There seems to be some kind of spell on him that won't let him do what he wants."

"Which may be why he can't give us a straight answer, either," added Renald thoughtfully. "You know, you may have something there."

Score looked from one to the other questioningly. "So now you think he's helping us?"

"Not necessarily," admitted Pixel. "But he's doing something. And whatever it is, we'll need to work it out, because he's obviously involved with our fate somehow. Whether on our side or against us I don't know yet." Then he grinned again. "I'll bet his real name is an anagram of those six letters, just like his fake names were."

"There's six letters," Score said. "That means there's 720 possible combinations of those letters. If we rule out the three he's already used, that still leaves us with 717 possible names. That's not much help."

"But if he is trying to be helpful," Pixel argued, "then one of the combinations must stand out above the rest. All we have to do is to play around with the letters and see if we can make a name out of them."

It seemed pointless to Score, but there didn't seem to be any use in complaining, so he started working on combinations of the letters: Realco, Elorac, Clorea, Olecra . . .

They continued on in silence for a while; Score stopped trying to unscramble LeCora's name. The others seemed lost in their own thoughts, which suited Score just fine. He found himself remembering his childhood, and they weren't memories he wanted to share with anyone. Even now, with danger stalking him, he felt happier than he had ever felt at home with Bad Tony. Even though he didn't much like them, he had to admit that Pixel and Renald were looking out for him. Maybe out of selfish reasons, but they were on his side.

He wasn't used to having people on his side.

He didn't know what to think anymore.

Dawn was breaking when they passed an area of burned-out trees. "Gee," Score muttered, "this looks awfully familiar."

"Looks like your handiwork," replied Pixel, with a slight grin. "The Tower can't be far now."

It wasn't. As they left the trees, they saw Aranak's Tower, glittering in the first rays of the day. It was still smoky glass, but the bright reds reflected in entrancing patterns against the blue Tower.

As they walked closer, Renald, Pixel, and Score could see a lone figure waiting for them.

Aranak.

He did not look pleased.

"Where have you been?" the wizard asked, in a voice that made Pixel shudder. "I've been so worried about you."

He did seem to be genuinely bothered, Score noticed. Maybe LeCora was wrong about him? Why would he be worried about them if he weren't their friend? "We're okay," Score told him.

"We were . . . captured by villagers," Pixel admitted.

That brought a fierce scowl to Aranak's face, and just a hint of fear to his eyes. "They got into my Tower?"

"Uh, no," Renald said slowly. "We got out. We wanted . . . some fresh air."

"Fresh air?" Aranak snorted. "You wanted to try your own magical abilities, that's what you wanted." Seeing their guilty expressions, he added, "I know you took those three books of magic. That's why I left them there. I had to see if you were really interested in your abilities, or were just humoring me." He seemed to be reining in his anger. "Actually, I'm quite impressed that you managed to figure out how to leave the Tower without having to ask me. Why don't we go and have some breakfast, and you can tell me what happened to you."

They re-entered the Tower by rapping on the wall, and for once Aranak joined them for a meal, though he didn't eat anything. "I already had my breakfast," he explained. "I was getting ready to join the Bestials in searching the woods for you. Now—what happened?"

Pixel told most of the story, since he was the talkative one among them. He told Aranak about the wolves, and of being captured, and their escape. Something then stirred inside Score, and he jumped in and finished quickly: "And that's it. We've been walking back all night." He felt that it would be a mistake to mention Relcoa. To his surprise, he saw that Pixel and Renald were nodding in agreement with him. They obviously felt the same way. If Aranak was their enemy, then talking about Relcoa would warn him. If he wasn't, then they would deal with Relcoa.

Aranak looked at them all with unhappy surprise he could barely conceal. "Fire?" he asked with an edge in his voice. "You conjured fire?"

Pixel nodded.

"You are not supposed to—how did you learn to conjure fire?" the wizard inquired.

"It was in one of the books," Score bluffed. But immediately he regretted his lie. Aranak, he sensed, knew the truth.

"I see," the wizard nodded and, from his expression, Renald, Pixel, and Score feared he saw too much.

Aranak was not going to dwell on their transgression. Instead, he said he was sure they must be exhausted. They had worked impressively. Now they needed rest.

Score felt confused by Aranak's compliment; he wondered whether it was a good thing or a bad thing to have impressed Aranak. He and the others rose to their feet. Aranak was right, he was feeling kind of sleepy. On the other hand, he also wanted to chat with Pixel and Renald. There were a few things on his mind. He could see that they all seemed to have the same thoughts. As they headed down the corridor to their rooms, Score said, "You guys want to come in for a minute?"

"Yes," Renald said. Pixel nodded, and they both joined Score in his room.

When the door was closed, Score said, "So, what did you think of that?"

"I think it was smart not to mention Oracle," Pixel said. "I just have a feeling it would have been a mistake."

"Oracle? Who's Oracle?" Score asked.

"Did I just say 'Oracle'?" Pixel seemed genuinely confused. "I meant Relcoa."

"No," Renald interrupted, "You meant Oracle. That's his real name, isn't it? The letters fit."

"But how did you know?" Score faced Pixel.

"I just said it. I didn't know it until I said it," Pixel explained.

"There are strange forces at work here," Renald observed. "And that's what bothers me. Why did all three of us feel that we shouldn't mention Oracle to Aranak? Is that what Oracle wanted us to think?"

"There's one way to find out," Pixel replied, smiling shyly. "If we're right, and we know his name, I'll bet we can call him to us. It can't be harder than calling the wolves was."

"Yeah, but that wasn't exactly the hour of our greatest triumph," Score pointed out. "What if this fails as well? We might bring in an army of the undead or something."

Renald gave him a scornful look. "I might have known you'd be too scared to try."

Score felt his face redden. "I didn't say I was chickening out," he protested. "I was just making a cautionary point."

"Point taken," Pixel said hastily, to stop further arguments. "So, let's do it, and see if we can get it right this time. Everyone concentrate on Oracle's name and his appearance, and I'll recite his name in the inverted alphabet."

Closing his eyes, Score focused his thoughts on the stranger and pictured his bizarre costume in his mind. He could hear Pixel call out softly, "LIZXOV." Then he again felt that little twist inside of him that told him something was working. When he opened his eyes, Oracle was standing there, beaming at them.

My confidence was not misplaced.
You've called me out of time and space.

"All right!" breathed Pixel, happily. "We got it right, then. Your real name is Oracle."

Oracle nodded, and looked at them the way that Score had always imagined a father might look on a child who pleased him. It wasn't a feeling he'd ever felt before.

Now you must be upon your guard,
For fate is pressing upon you hard.
Seek out your book, but in reverse,
Before your fate gets any worse.

And then he was gone.

"Well," Score commented cynically, "that didn't tell us much, did it?"

"It told us that we were right about Oracle," Pixel replied. "And we can now summon him when we want him, instead of waiting for him to pop up."

Score shrugged. "Yeah, but he still goes when he feels like it, and won't give us a straight answer."

"Then we'll have to work on those parts," Pixel replied.

"We have to seek the Book of Names. I'm feeling more and more certain that our fates are somehow bound up with it," said Renald.

"Female intuition," Score couldn't help sneering in response.

"Would you rather have a female fist in the mouth?" asked Renald, sweetly.

"Break it up," Pixel said. "Let's get some rest, then meet in the dining room in a few hours. We'll all feel better then."

Once the others were gone, Score threw himself onto his bed. He, too, was tired and needed some sleep. But there was an odd warmth inside him. It looked like some people were actually concerned about his welfare at last. Pixel and Renald, for two. He found he was getting less and less irritated with them. He just hoped he wasn't actually starting to like them.

And Oracle had seemed to be proud of him. That was kind of a two-edged sword, though. He wasn't sure he trusted Oracle, so his approval didn't mean much. Except it had felt good to be looked at that way for once in his life.

And Aranak had seemed to be genuinely worried about them, as well as impressed with what they'd done. He had promised them something special later, and that sounded like it could be fun. If Aranak could be trusted.

All in all, despite the problems still ahead, Score felt pretty good about his life.

At least, he did while he slept.

11

Renald woke up feeling refreshed. She'd slept maybe three hours, but it had been enough for her. She was used to her strenuous life. She sat up on her bed and pulled her tunic back over her head, reaching automatically for the cap that was no longer there. She still felt almost naked without it, but there didn't seem to be much she could do about it. Oddly enough, she actually felt better now, knowing that Score and Pixel knew the truth about her and that it hadn't bothered them too much. Well, Pixel, at least. Score was another matter.

She had seen something in his eyes when he had thought about his past. It was a haunted look, like the ones she'd seen in the eyes of dogs that had been brutalized by their owners. As if a simple faith and love had been battered out of them by unjust treatment and betrayal. Score was obviously a more complex person than she'd given him credit for being. Maybe Pixel was right, and she should be less harsh with him.

Pixel. Oddly enough, she discovered she quite liked the skinny youth. Despite his appalling lack of real skills, he had courage and he was quick-witted. Again, her initial estimate of him was proving to be inaccurate. Was she losing her touch? Or was it just that you couldn't judge everyone by the standards of a warrior? She didn't know, but she'd have to think about it.

And then she realized something else. She no longer had her cap, of course, and now let her hair hang free about her shoulders. She definitely looked female, and not at all male. Yet Aranak hadn't seemed to notice. Had he always known she was a girl? Interesting . . . Someone must have known. On

Score's piece of paper, it clearly indicated two males and one female, joined together. That had to refer to the three of them.

She went to the dining room and picked at some of the food there, waiting until Pixel and Score showed up together. They were also lost in their thoughts and ate sparingly. For once, Score simply ate the food instead of changing it. When they were done, she stood up.

"I think it's time we looked for the Book of Magic," she said simply.

"But where?" asked Pixel. "If it's so valuable, then Aranak's bound to keep it hidden away. He must have a secret chamber somewhere where it's stored."

"Not necessarily," said Score, with a grin. "You guys have probably never heard of Edgar Allan Poe, but he wrote a very famous story on our world. It's called 'The Purloined Letter.' It's about a man who hides a very important letter, and nobody can find it until the detective realizes where it is. It's hidden in plain sight, with other unimportant letters. It was the best possible hiding site."

Pixel gave a wide grin. "So you think that Aranak would hide his most valuable book in with his unimportant ones—in his library."

"Right," agreed Score, smugly. "I'm sure I'm right."

"You could be," agreed Renald. There was certainly something to be said for that theory. "But my father hides his valuables away in a guarded, locked room. Maybe Aranak does, too."

"There aren't any guards in the Tower," Score pointed out. "Just him and us."

"He can do magic," Renald replied. "He doesn't need a living guard." That wiped the grins off their faces. "Let's do this logically, shall we? Like an armed raid. After all, we are trying to get something he most likely wouldn't want us to have."

"So you think he's our enemy, then?" asked Pixel, concerned.

"I don't know," Renald answered. "But he seems very jealous of his magical secrets. I don't think he wants to share any important ones with us in case we prove to be stronger than he is. That seems to scare him. Don't forget, he told us himself he stays here to steer clear of stronger magicians. Also, I think he'd turn on someone to save his own skin, and expects us to do the same. That's why I want to get that book now. I have a feeling it will bring us further instruction."

"Makes sense," agreed Pixel. "Right, let's go."

The library was back in place again, so they could simply walk inside. It looked perfectly normal, just as it had when they were doing their lessons. Renald looked around the room. There were dozens of bookcases and thousands and thousands of books. "This search could take us a long time," she said with a sigh. "And Aranak is going to be looking for us soon."

"But what are we looking for?" asked Score. "Can't we narrow it down a bit?"

"Oracle said something about looking for our book in reverse," Pixel said. "Whatever that means."

"It's all been a kind of play on words so far," Renald said slowly. "And magic is all about knowing the right names for things. I suspect that's how the book we want is being hidden."

Pixel laughed. "I'll bet you're correct," he agreed. "And looking for it in reverse must mean that the title is reversed. So we should look for a book that's called something like 'Cigam fo Koob,' for 'Book of Magic.'"

Score frowned. "Hang on," he muttered. "I remember seeing a book like that the other day." He concentrated hard. "It was in the adventure stories section."

"A perfect place to hide it," said Renald, admiringly. "Anyone looking for it would think it was just a silly adventure story." She followed Score as he led the way to the right section of the bookcases. Her hands were tingling, as if they were drawing close to something they wanted to hold. "This has got to be it," she said softly. Without even looking at the titles, she drew out one of the books, which seemed to fit perfectly into her hand. "Cigam Fo Koob Eht," it read. "The Book of Magic" reversed.

She flipped open the book, and a sheet of paper fell out, drifting toward the floor. She caught it before it reached the carpet, and then examined it. Score and Pixel stared over her shoulders.

It looked similar to the page that Score had shown them earlier. And it was just as confusing. The only thing familiar about it was the $111 > 1 + 1 + 1$, again. It made no more sense this time around.

"Great," she muttered. "Instead of one page we don't understand, now we have two."

"We should be able to figure it out," Pixel insisted. "We just need time." He stared at the line of odd letters. " LOIRSATCELNE . . ." he mused. "I wonder if that's some kind of code? Like the earlier one, with reversed alphabet? That would make it . . . O—L—R—H—Z—" he broke off. "That makes even less sense. Must be something else, then."

be garware man
gar beman ware
LOIRSATCELNE
G.T. T.H. H.R.T. F. T.H.
DDM
RELEASE
corrupted at the core. Yo
man has taken over. cff y

"What about these dots, above and below the letters?" asked Renald. "They alternate, up and down. Could they be a clue?"

Pixel grinned. "I think you've got it," he said. "Alternate letters. If we take alternate letters, then we get . . . L—I —S—T—E—N. That's 'listen'! And the next bit reads . . . O—R—A—C—L—E. 'Listen Oracle!'"

Score snorted. "Does that mean we should listen to what he says?" he asked. "Frankly, I'm not in favor of that." He returned to scanning the titles of the books on the shelf. "Hey, here's another book like that!" He held it up. The title was *Seman Fo Koob Eht*. "'The Book of Names.' I wonder what it could be."

Renald folded up her sheet of paper and slipped it back inside the cover of the Book of Magic. As she did so, she noticed that there was a small bookplate inside the cover. It showed a pair of entwined serpents and the words "Property of Eremin." Who was Eremin? Maybe it was just a book Aranak had collected from somewhere. Then she slipped the book into her travel pack and went to join Score.

This new book was even odder than the previous one. On the cover was a mirror below the title. Was this significant? Score opened the page, and they all stared in confusion at the odd lettering inside.

RENALD IS HELAINE
DERLETH IS SAMAOS
WALKER IS CRAIG
ARANAK IS DARTHCOURT
PRIOR IS JENNIFER
ROOTHMAN IS CHA

“It looks like modern art or something,” Score complained. “I don’t get it.”

“It’s obviously in some kind of code, again,” Pixel, pointed out. “We just have to figure out what sort of code.”

“Maybe each shape stands for a letter?” Renald suggested. “A substitution code.”

“Perhaps,” Pixel said, but he didn’t sound too certain. “Or maybe it’s something else?” He stared at the book for a moment. “There’s a mirror on the cover,” he said slowly. “Maybe that’s a clue?”

“Mirror writing?” suggested Score. “There’s a thought.” He glanced around the room and saw a mirror hanging in an alcove. “Let’s try it.” He held the page up to the mirror and frowned. "It looks just the same," he complained. "Weird."

"Not weird," Pixel said, excitedly. "It means that the book is already mirrored. What the writer has done is to take a letter and also its mirror image and join them together. That's why it looks so odd. To read it, we just have to cover up the righthand side of the figures!" He examined the page they were on. "Then this reads: 'Derleth is Samaos.'"

"Terrific," Score said. "And that tells us precisely nothing."

A suspicion was forming in Renald's mind. "Maybe not," she said, slowly. "This is the Book of Names, right? And Aranak said that you need to know a person's real name in order to do magic on them."

Pixel nodded excitedly. "Then this is his list of people's real names!" he agreed. He flipped through the book until he came to an early page. "Here's the A section. Let's see if his own name is in here . . ." A few moments later, he laughed. "'Aranak is Darthcort,'" he read. "That's what we needed!"

At that second, Renald felt a strange sensation. It was like a twisting inside of her stomach, and then, suddenly, her body was a huge mass of pain. She heard both Pixel and Score cry out, and realized that whatever was affecting her must be attacking them also. There were lights flashing, but she couldn't tell whether they were inside or outside her head.

She felt herself falling forward. There must have been a spell guarding the Book of Names, she thought to herself. And we must have set it off.

12

Pixel tried to move and discovered that he couldn't. He felt as if he'd been set in some sort of plastic, utterly unable to move a muscle of his body. He had a moment of panic, wondering if he'd somehow been paralyzed, before realizing that he could open his eyes.

He almost wished he couldn't. He could now see Score and Renald, both seated beside him, and both obviously as helpless as he was.

They were no longer inside the Tower but on the meadow in front of it, before the forest began. All around them were gathered maybe a hundred of the Bestials. In front of them stood Aranak, a smug grin on his face, and the Book of Names in his hands. He made a gesture and the book vanished.

S'hee stepped forward. He looked almost ashamed, but resolute at the same time. "You must go on," he informed them. "The Shadows have ordered that you be sacrificed to the Gateway. If you are not, we shall be punished."

"What are these Shadows?" asked Renald.

"They are the dark servants of the ruling powers of the Diadem," S'hee replied. "They have commanded your sacrifice, and we cannot disobey."

Craning his neck slightly, Pixel could just make out the black slash in space that marked the edge of a Gateway.

"I don't understand," Renald said to Aranak. "Why have you helped us until now?"

Aranak sighed. "Dear girl, I haven't helped you that much, and I had my reasons. Do you recall that I told you I had to stay on this world because if I traveled to the Middle Circuit of the Diadem, the magic there would probably rip me apart?"

"Yes."

"Well, there's a way around that," Aranak answered. "All I need to do is to siphon off your powers to add to my own. The reason I trained you as I did was to see whether you really did have magical power that I could tap. I have to admit that I was surprised at just how much you do have. If I had taught you much longer, you'd have become more powerful than I."

Rahn stepped forward, her catlike face scowling. "No!" she insisted. "You cannot defy the Shadows. They must be sacrificed."

"I am not wasting their power!" Aranak snapped. "And I'm not afraid of the Shadows."

Pixel was still scared. "What will happen to us if you take our power?" he demanded.

"You?" Aranak looked as though he hadn't thought about it. "I'm afraid it will kill you, of course. But you'll be giving to a worthy cause." He smirked.

"No!" cried Renald, struggling again to free herself. "Face us like a man! Let me have my sword!" Pixel saw that her scabbard was empty.

"You must be joking," laughed Aranak. "Young lady, you'll stay where you are until I'm finished with you."

"No!" yelled Rahn, and she leaped for him, her claws and fangs ready to rip out his throat.

Aranak made a gesture, and the leopard-woman simply hung suspended in the air, frozen in place several feet from the ground. "So melodramatic," he muttered.

Pixel was astonished. He realized then that all of the other Bestials seemed to be frozen in place. "What have you done to them?" he asked.

And then, suddenly, realization and hope filled Pixel. Aranak didn't know his name!

Pixel wasn't his true name! It was his online name. He used it so much that he didn't really think about it. But his true name was Shalar.

My name is Shalar, he told himself. Not Pixel! Shalar isn't held by this spell! Over and over again he repeated this to himself, over and over. It had to work! It had to! Or they were all dead . . .

And then he could move his right hand. With a grin, he pushed forward. Now his left hand was free, too. With rising confidence, the spell was growing weaker. He could feel the chains of it snapping as he struggled to his feet.

Aranak looked up from his book, startled and shaken. "No!" he exclaimed. "It's not possible! You can't possibly break that binding spell!"

"Yes, I can," Pixel snarled, elation flowing through him. "You don't know my true name at all."

"Nor mine," growled Renald, staggering to her feet.

"Or mine," finished Score, rising to join them, "You're finished, you dirty liar!"

"No!" screamed Aranak. "I shall still win! I have the spell to drain you—now!" He spoke a few words, and gestured with his hand.

Pixel could feel the magic tearing at him, like a hurricane, slamming into him and wrenching at his soul. In a moment of unbearable agony, he felt the power ripping into his heart and soul, attempting to drag the life force out of him.

"Fight it," Pixel gasped. "He can't defeat us! He doesn't have our true names!" Even as he said this, some of the pressure seemed to ease. He stared through his pain-darkened eyes at Aranak, who was now visibly on the brink of panic.

"If I can't drain you," he snarled, "then I'll kill you!" With a gesture, he threw up his hands—and the world changed! Pixel felt a searing coldness close about him, and water all around. He struggled to breathe, knowing he was sinking into inky waters. His lungs felt as if they were going to burst, and he could see nothing at all in the blackness. He had to fight against the panic welling up inside him. Somehow,

Aranak had transported him into the ocean—and probably Score and Renald, too. What could he do to get out of this? He couldn't think, he couldn't even breathe . . .

And then the water was gone, though it was still pitch black. Thankfully, Pixel took a deep breath, and felt his tension relaxing slightly.

"You guys okay?" came Score's voice from a few feet away.

"Yes," said Renald, coughing slightly.

"What happened?" asked Pixel, still unable to make anything out.

Score chuckled. "I always knew watching TV would pay off one day," he commented. "I just pictured a force shield around me, like they use on Star Trek, and—bingo! It worked!"

Pixel couldn't quite follow the logic of this, but he let it pass. "You can keep it going okay?" he asked.

"Well," Score admitted, "it's a strain, and I don't think I can keep it up for long. So will you two please think of some way out of this?"

Before they could even think, they were out of the water.

And falling.

Pixel glanced down, and was almost sick. They had been transported high into the air, and were dropping fast toward the ground below them. His body was shaking, partly from fear and partly from the cold air whipping past them.

"Do something!" Score groaned. "I'm keeping the shield in place, but I don't think it'll help us to bounce."

Pixel tried to concentrate. Renald was shaking, clearly terribly afraid. Of course—she was from a world where flying was unknown. It was up to him to think of a way out . . . And fast! Parachutes? No, they were too complicated, and he wasn't sure if he could figure out the strings and stuff properly. He knew that a bad parachute was worse than no chute at all.

Then . . . He grinned as it came to him. Carefully, he formed the image in his mind, praying that it would work. The ground was heading in their direction terribly fast. Then he felt the magic flow.

Instantly, all three of them were wearing hang gliders. The sail above him billowed and caught, and he was suddenly floating instead of falling. He couldn't direct the glider, but that hardly mattered. Their falls had stopped, and they were now safe. Score gave a strained laugh of encouragement, and even Renald managed a shaky smile.

This was almost fun . . .

And then everything changed again. Aranak must have known they'd survived that death trap, and struck again.

This time, the three of them were on solid ground, their hang gliders weighing them down. Pixel managed to make them vanish as he tried to get his bearings.

Then the ground shook, throwing him off balance. Before he could regain it, the ground shook again, and then shattered.

"Earthquake!" yelled Renald, and Pixel realized she was right. The ground was thrumming under his feet, and he saw a crack start to form. Aranak was trying to kill them in a quake!

The ground split, and Pixel had a momentary glimpse of a deep chasm opening. His mind refused to work, and he knew that they were all going to be plunged into the earth and die . . .

Would Score's force-shield save them? Pixel doubted it. If the fall didn't kill them, then the tremors and the moving ground would crush them to death. The ground shook again, throwing them all to the ground.

As he stared in horror, a massive slice in the earth started to open beneath them. With grim certainty, Pixel knew they were going to die.

And then they were all three floating several inches above the ground. The shaking had ceased now that they were no longer in contact with the earth, and the crack passed harmlessly beneath them. Pixel knew he hadn't done anything, so he glanced at Renald.

"It was all I could think of," she said. "To get off the ground."

He grinned at her. "And it worked. The quakes can't affect us now."

Then he felt the grip of magic about him, as they were again transported—out of the shaking lands—

And into something far, far worse.

All about them was molten lava, blazing hot and burning its way through solid rock. Aranak had plunged them into the heart of a volcano!

Pixel could see the other two very well now, both looking as wet and bedraggled as he felt. The heat was starting to mount in their little bubble, but obviously Score's force shield was somehow still holding up. Pixel could see the expression of agony on the other boy's face, though.

"Hurry!" Score gasped. "I can't hold this together for much longer."

Globs of molten lava sizzled and seethed past them. Pixel concentrated on thinking of a way out. "If we can bring Aranak here," he suggested, "then we can latch on to whatever he uses to get himself out of here."

"Good idea," Renald agreed. "Assuming the lava doesn't kill him."

"It's his trap," Pixel pointed out. "He'd hardly be stupid enough to let it kill him, too."

"Just do it," gasped Score. He was starting to crack.

Renald nodded. Then, softly, she said to Pixel, "We have to kill Aranak. Otherwise, he will certainly kill us. I do not really wish to do it, but we have no option."

Pixel knew what she meant. He wished there was another way out, but Aranak was clearly not going to give up. "How can we kill him?" he asked. "He's got years of magic practice on us."

"True," agreed Renald. "But we can do it without magic. You saw how scared of my sword he was."

"But you don't have it now," Pixel objected.

"No," Renald agreed. "But he didn't search me when he had the chance. Fatal mistake." She pulled a long, slender dagger from inside her boot. "Now—how do we get him here?"

"Hurry!" yelled Score.

"The calling spell," Pixel answered quickly. "We know his real name is Darthcourt. All we have to do is use the spell and say his name using the backward alphabet."

Nodding, Renald concentrated. Pixel did the same, picturing the spell. Then, together, they called, "WZIGSXLFIG!"

And, outside their spell-maintained force-shield, Aranak suddenly blinked into existence. He looked startled, and then irritated, and finally downright scared. He muttered something under his breath, and Pixel focused in on it. It had to be the spell he was using to return to the Tower. Pixel pictured the three of them hitching a ride on the same spell . . .

Suddenly they were back in the clearing in front of the Tower. Once again, Aranak looked stunned at what they had done. Score gasped, and collapsed forward, obviously almost entirely drained of strength. The force-shield dissolved around them.

"Why won't you just die?" screamed Aranak. He threw up his hands in another gesture, and then the earth all about them exploded into frenzy. Tendrils whipped up from the ground, wrapping about them. Growing at a terrific rate, the plants whirled about the three of them, and then started tightening their vise-like grips. Pixel's circulation was being cut off, and he couldn't breathe. He had to get out of this fast!

No. There was something more important than his escape. Renald had to be able to stop Aranak, which meant he had to free Renald before freeing himself—if he could stand it. Fighting the pain and the urge to panic, Pixel focused his mind on the tendrils holding Renald. He fought to be as precise as he could and then formed the image of the plants' coils burning. Carefully, so as not to burn Renald as well, he focused his energies.

In puffs of smoke, the tendrils of the plants started to burn and fall off, leaving Renald shaking, gasping, and ready for action. A red haze of agony was sweeping over Pixel's vision, as he started to succumb. But he saw Renald's arm whip back, and then forward.

With a loud cry, Aranak froze in place, staring down at the knife that was now buried in his chest. His eyes went wide in shock and terror, and then he started to collapse forward.

As he did so, the plants about Pixel and Score crumbled to dust and fell, as well. Pixel crumpled to the ground, barely able to breathe or see. He could just make out a flare of light around Aranak's body, though, and the magician's corpse vanished.

"We're still alive," breathed Score, getting to his knees. He looked more dead than alive, but, like Pixel, he was getting stronger with every passing moment.

"Yes," agreed Renald. "Thanks to you. You helped save our lives, Score. Thank you."

Score actually looked embarrassed. "It was an accident," he said. "I had to save you both to save myself. Believe me, I'm not likely to do it again."

"Probably not," agreed Renald. But she was still smiling as she said it. She didn't believe Score any more than Pixel had.

Rahn, S'hee, and Hakar came forward, looking even more confused than the three friends. "What . . . what has happened to Aranak?" Rahn asked.

"He's gone," Pixel informed the Bestials. "Dead."

Rahn nodded, and then glanced at the still-open Gateway. "You must go through," she said, firmly.

"Hold it, furball," said Score, annoyed. "We don't have to do anything we don't want to do. You heard Aranak. We've got the power. We can take over his Tower, too. You don't get rid of us that easily."

Rahn's face fell as she realized that this was true. "But . . . but if you do not go, we will be punished," she said, almost whining.

"Tough," muttered Score. "That's not our problem."

Pixel shook his head. "Yes, it is," he insisted. "Look, Aranak didn't care about anyone else. But I can't just stand by and see these people punished when we can prevent it." He stared at the Gateway. "And there's something within me that tells me this is the way we should go."

"It could get us killed," Score complained.

Pixel snorted. "So far, we've almost been killed several times on this world. What can they do worse on another?"

Smiling almost proudly, Renald asked, "Are you sure you want to find out?"

"No," he admitted honestly. "But do we have a choice?"

"I don't think so," she agreed. "We are the warriors here. We are the only ones who stand a chance. And Aranak said that on the next level we would be stronger. If we have to fight these Shadows, we'll probably need all the power we can get. Besides," she eyed the Bestials coldly, "I think I've had about as much of these . . . people as I can take. Let them have their peace."

Rahn looked at them in amazement. "You would do this willingly?" she asked. "Sacrifice yourselves to save us?"

Score snorted. "Hey, whoever is on the other side of that Gateway had better start worrying," he said. "If they mess with us, they're going to have trouble. Right?" He looked at Renald and Pixel.

"Right," they chorused.

The Bestials shook their heads, puzzled and yet somehow proud. Rahn reached into the small strip of cloth she wore at her waist and drew out a tiny bag. "You are all very brave," she said, clearly impressed. "Because you are so concerned, take these."

Pixel did so. "What are they?"

"Gemstones," Hakar informed them. "We know that magic-users can increase their powers if they focus them through jewels. They will help you wherever you go." He looked embarrassed. "I am sorry you must part from us like this, but we shall remember you."

Pixel nodded. "Thanks." He put the gems into his pocket. On the next world, he'd examine them and see what they could do. He knew the Bestials were only being generous because they felt guilty. Well, they were guilty. It was hard to feel too sorry for them, or too affectionate. He turned to his companions. "Are you ready to go?"

"One further thing," Hakar said. He held out his hands, and Renald grinned widely.

"My sword!" She snatched it from him and slid it into her sheath. She gestured to the Bestials to stand back. Then she turned to face Pixel and Score. "I'm not very good at saying I'm sorry," she said slowly. "Or saying that I'm wrong. But I am sorry, and I was wrong about both of you. You're not such cowards after all. You both proved yourselves." She winced and then added, "And my real name is Helaine."

Pixel was shocked, both by the apology and the revelation. "You just told us your name, he said. "You've given us power over you."

"I know," she said calmly. "I believe I can trust you." She held out her hand.

Pixel took it. "I'm Shalar," he replied, touched deeply.

Score groaned, and then held out his hand.

"Geez, you two make a production out of everything, don't you? I'm Matt. Now can we get going?"

Pixel and Renald nodded, grinning. "Let's go," said Pixel, feeling braver than he had for a long time. Knowing that his friends were following him, he stepped into the Gateway . . .

To where?

EPILOGUE

The Shadows writhed and laughed as they watched what was happening in the scrying pool. Everything was going perfectly according to their Master's plans.

"Fools," murmured their Master, happily. "Now I know their true names—Helaine, Shalar, and Matt. And if they thought that this amateur Aranak was tough . . . wait until they meet me."

He laughed to himself, and the Shadows joined in, their eerie voices echoing around the halls. The trio's problems had only just begun . . .

The story continues in
BOOK OF SIGNS

To Write to the Author

If you wish to contact the author, please write to the author in care of Llewellyn Worldwide, and we will forward your letter. Both the author and publisher appreciate hearing from you and learning of your enjoyment of this book. Llewellyn Worldwide cannot guarantee that every letter written to the author can be answered, but all will be forwarded. Please write to:

John Peel
% Llewellyn Worldwide
P.O. Box 64383, Dept. 0-7387-0617-5
St. Paul, MN 55164-0383, U.S.A., Earth, The Diadem

Please enclose a self-addressed stamped envelope, or one dollar to cover costs. If outside U.S.A., enclose international postal reply coupon.

Many of Llewellyn's authors have Web sites with additional information and resources. For more information, please visit our Web site at:

http://www.llewellyn.com

Llewellyn Worldwide does not participate in, endorse, or have any authority or responsibility concerning private business transactions between our authors and the public.

CHECK OUT THE REST OF THE DIADEM SERIES BY JOHN PEEL

Follow along as the adventures of Score, Helaine, and Pixel continue. The Diadem is a dangerous place and the trio of young magic-users is only beginning to discover its perils. Powerful magic forces are drawing the kids to the center of the Diadem for a thrilling final showdown.

BOOK OF SIGNS

In the second book of the Diadem series, Score, Helaine, and Pixel find themselves on Rawn, where they must put their powers to use to fight off goblins, trolls, and a giant lake monster. The three young wizards also befriend centaurs and learn to use magical gemstones. All the while, a mysterious force continues to draw them closer to the center of the Diadem and to their destiny.

ISBN 0-7387-0616-7 $4.99

Book of Magic

The third book of the series begins on Dondar, one world away from the center of the Diadem. The kids make friends with unicorns, who prove to be valuable allies. But as they are swept off Dondar to Jewel, the center of the Diadem, the three must work together if they are to pass the ultimate test, as they face Sarman and the Triad, the forces that have been drawing them to this final showdown from the very beginning.

ISBN 0-7387-0615-9 $4.99

Book of Thunder

The Triad may be vanquished and the Diadem secured, but Score, Pixel, and Helaine are not out of trouble. The unicorns are in danger and Thunder has been vanquished. Only the three can figure out who or what is controlling the unicorn herd and save Thunder.

ISBN 0-7387-0614-0 $4.99

Where would you like to go?

Got ideas?

Llewellyn would love to know what kinds of books you are looking for but just can't seem to find. Fantasy, witchy, occult, science fiction, or just plain scary—what do you want to read? What types of books speak specifically to you? If you have ideas, suggestions, or comments, write Megan at:

megana@llewellyn.com

Llewellyn Publications
Attn: Megan, Acquisitions
P.O. Box 64383
St. Paul, MN 55164-0383 USA
1-800-THE MOON (1-800-843-6666)
www.llewellyn.com